T0348693

The Queens' Ball

Copi

The Queens' Ball

A NOVEL

TRANSLATED FROM THE FRENCH
BY KIT SCHLUTER

WITH AN AFTERWORD, INDEX, AND NOTES
BY THIBAUD CROISY
TRANSLATED BY OLIVIA BAES

Mercurial Editions, 2024
An Imprint of Inpatient Press

Contents

for Marielle de Lesseps

1

Pietro Gentiluomo

This is the third time in a year that I've started writing this novel the subject of which mustn't be very interesting to me, whenever I finish a notebook (I always write with a Bic pen in a spiral notebook) I lose it the very same day. And seeing as I forget everything that I write, I have to start over from zero. My editor throws a fit at me. He's given me an advance on this novel far surpassing any amount I'll ever make from its sale. These fits have been part of our relationship for its first decade, they're completely unrelated to the book's success. My editor pushes me to write. He asked me for my first book of drawings before I'd even drawn enough to fill a pamphlet. One day, I told him to go see Gombrowicz's *Ivona, Princess of Burgundy*, staged by Lavelli. And so began his passion for theater. He gave me an advance on my first plays, which he published before they had a director or actors. I published my first novel, which he loved, but which flopped. That didn't deter him. He asked me for a follow-up. What's more, I live off these advances, if he managed to break even on them he'd get nervous, he's worried I'll stop writing. The novel I was going to write (I say going to because I'm doing it now) was a different one: it was a novel about travestis, because I so enjoy coming up with situations to place them in, but I've already done that in my plays, it's nicer than in a novel where you don't see anything, and the travesti deserves to be seen. Whatever the case, I did come up with a few who were always working the Carrefour de Buci, probably because this neighborhood used to be host to some of the most interesting ones among them. But then the Carrefour de Buci started taking control of my imagination, my three travestis got surrounded by, and soon lost among, other characters: sex kittens, hoodlums, cops. Soon Buci had spread to Saint-Germain-des-Prés and my characters began to mingle with the antique dealers on Rue Jacob and the shop workers on Rue de Rennes, then they all started mingling together. Between Place de la Contrescarpe and Rue du Bac, between the Fourteenth Arrondissement and the Seine (with an outcropping in the Marais), I was left with too vast a territory populated by sketchily-defined characters, plus the tourists. And amidst all that was my editor, always, comfortably esconced in his fortress between Saint-Sulpice and Le Sénat, waiting for the tip of my pen to keep him informed of the state of the people, on which my courtier's fee depended. I swear. But whose idea was it? For starters, who's going to buy the book? He must think: the very type of people I'm writing about. People who buy a book because they feel like it concerns them personally (an oh-so-precious few) or their professional habits or neighborhoods (three or four-thousand people) or, in the best case scenario, in a more affordable edition, people who take an interest in everything, particularly in crime. Lord knows he isn't dreaming of it becoming a bestseller. No, he'd be afraid of losing me. He's worried that if I get rich I'll become an editor myself and poach all his authors (the dream of every author is to have an editor-author who does his work for him), stranding him and obligating him in turn to write for a living. His nightmare goes so far as to make him imagine that he'll be forced to pen his memoirs to survive, I'm his editor and I refuse to pay him an advance until he's finished, but he's never able to write the last page, so difficult are the books he published (to each of which he devotes a chapter) to recount, so difficult his motivations for publishing them to express. He wakes with a start and scrawls on a piece of paper: Don't forget to ask Copi for his novel. Then he goes back to sleep. But what novel? I've lost the beginnings of two, of which I recall only fragments: Pierre on the terrace of a café chatting with a travesti about Yves Saint Laurent's

Moroccan-style capes, summer 1969; Pierre and I at a hippie party, both dressed up as Marie Antionette, Ibiza, 1971. I wonder why Pierre looms so large in this novel, because Pierre actually exists, he's my friend in real life; what's so unreal about him to make him the only living being capable of slipping so easily into my imagination alongside the fictional characters? When, suddenly, disaster strikes: Pierre dies. And the novel writes itself in the pain his death causes me, feeding off my pain. My editor doesn't deserve this much. I tell him so, too. You're not exempt from life's blows, he tells me. But were you really so attached to him? He's the only person I've ever truly been in love with, I say. But he was kind of stupid, he replies. Sure, he was stupid, it's true, but he was very handsome. An Italian from the South with almond eyes, his real name was Pietro Gentiluomo. I picked him up at the Vatican Museum a good ten years ago, he was there drawing the Egyptian mummies, he touched up photos to put on postcards, that was his job. The next day he was introducing me to his mom, a movie theater usherette. They invited me over for risotto in a little two-bedroom flat in Trastevere where his mom showed me pictures of Pierre's dad, a film actor who died in the studio fire on the Cinecittà set that killed five hundred people while she was still pregnant with Pierre. Disturbed by this tragedy, Pierre refused to appear in films despite the countless offers he received due to his physical beauty. Il cinema porta disgrazia, he said, his mother nodding along beside him. He stuffed his face like an ogre, talking endlessly and waving his fork in the air. A Parigi si vive bene? Qui a Roma è la provincia. Napoli è bella, si, ma pericolosa. He made fashion drawings. He showed me an album full of colorful sketches of chubby girls squeezed into lamé with long skirts slit up to their waistlines and flowers in their hair, of rather tropical inspiration. He drew nothing but evening dresses. And he dreamed of Paris. First I invited him to see Venice, which he'd never visited. His mom entrusted him to me (ve la raccomando, signore!) a thousand times over on the doorstep, her eyes brimming with tears. Even though I was hardly older than Pierre (I was twenty-five at the time, he was eighteen), she already saw me as a sort of godfather figure. The mother and son's farewells were never-ending and emotional. She ran after the car waving goodbye for some two-hundred feet, Pierre was crying too. We got to Venice one morning in the month of April, I was already in love. We took a room at a *pensione* hotel near Piazza San Marco, we walked around all day, ate and drank in excess, we made love and took a nap and before going out for dinner, Pierre wanted to call his mom at the Cinema Rex where she worked. She had died, burned alive alongside seven hundred spectators in a fire at the Rex the night before. Pierre wept, sobbed, prayed, pulled his hair out. From that day on, he never went into a movie theater again, and even took measures to avoid passing in front of one. Simple conversations about film were painful for him, he didn't know who Marilyn Monroe was. We returned to Rome that same night. We buried his mom in the little cemetery in Marinella not far from Rome, where his dad already lay buried. We can't tell if the body they show us is the right one, it's so charred. He'd had the same doubt about his dad's body, it's possible that the two corpses lying there together in that minuscule tomb never actually met during their lifetimes and that all the tears that Pierre shed on the gravestone were addressed to perfect strangers. I had to make a stop in Milan to see my dear friends the Gandinis before returning to Paris, I brought him with me. He made an atrocious impression on the Milanese editors I introduced him to, he behaved poorly at the table and spoke of nothing but the fires in which his mother and father had perished. As soon as he had an opportunity, Gandini took me aside and asked me: what do you see in him? The sex is good, I replied, to cut him off. How else could I explain interclass homosexuality to a Milanese editor, however close we may have been, in 1965? And has it really changed all that much? We stayed for two days in Milan, Pierre felt uncomfortable, so did I. As soon as I was able to post off my things we returned to Paris, instead of staying for the week I normally spent with my Milanese friends. Pierre moved into an apartment with me at 2 Boulevard Saint-German with three windows overlooking the Seine, and he loved it there.

It was in this apartment, which I still miss (I let my dad take it over), that I experienced Pierre's transformation. Not into a Parisian, but into a woman. And not gradually, but all at once.

But before I get into that, I should tell you about gay life back then around Saint-Germain. I'm familiar with it, my editor replies. You don't know a thing. Maybe you had dinner upstairs at Le Fiacre, but that's it. I, on the other hand, spent years cruising the bar downstairs before heading to the pissoirs and ending up at La Pergola in the small hours. And then it was off to the Tuileries, to make my first pickups who still stunk of aftershave. You're vulgar, my editor says. Besides, I can't cut you a check for ten thousand francs. My accountant's beside himself. I haven't made back any of the money I put into your last play. How many pages is that novel of yours going to be? I have no idea. Alright, I'll write you a check for five thousand, but don't ask me for any more this quarter. I'm awfully sorry about Pierre. I saw him with you at Chez Castel once. Pierre never stepped foot in Chez Castel. Then I must be confusing him with the another one of your boys, the Arab. I think your idea of writing a novel about gay men is a good one, you're so deeply acquainted with the subject. A novel about gay men? Pierre in a novel about gay men? I'm indignant. I storm out of my editor's place, my mind made up not to write the book. I run into ten, fifteen boutique queens on the sidewalk on Rue Bonaparte. I might know a few of them, I get them all mixed up. My future readers, I hiss to myself. No, they're not much for reading. But novels about queens? *Death in Venice*, maybe. In any event, they've never come to any of my plays. I check out the window display at a shoe shop on Rue du Four, each pair is more appalling than the last, I'm increasingly convinced that I shouldn't write this novel. I look up at the window of a garret where I used to live a good fifteen years back. Before Pierre. You're coming up with a novel all for yourself. Isn't this, I ask myself, why you've lost the start of two books, why you scorn the public's welcome before you've even received it, why you make scenes at your editor? What else could be as intimate as Pierre's novel? Pierre's body, I thought. The memory of Pierre's smell hit me as violently as an electroshock and the image of Pierre's corpse came to mind. I was so unhappy, I didn't know what to do with myself. Breakfast in Saint-Germain? The way home along Rue Saint-Benoit where I'd so often had dinner, cruised, performed in the café-theaters always depresses me. Marielle de Lesseps is sitting outside the Café de Flore. One of the only people I could have run into here and been happy to see. It sends me back ten years but as if no time had passed at all, and without regrets. It's true, she says, everyone's a monster here. I knew you'd just come back from the States and I knew I could find you at the Flore. I protest: it was by pure chance that I passed by. Was New York fun? I wasn't in New York, I was out in the countryside in Massachusetts. Staying with Julie Ann and Julian Cairol, whom she knows. What was I up to? Forgetting Pierre. Really, I was devastated. I started writing a novel twice and forgot one copy on a beach and the other at the airport in Boston. About Pierre. About Pierre? she asked, taken aback. But he was an absolute moron. I know. I cut myself off from my world because of him, none of my friends could stand him, but I was forced in turn to put up with his. Frankly, ten years was too long. It's for the best that he died. Let's go have a bite at Lipp. We're in a good mood; Marielle is able to play down Pierre's death long enough for us to have lunch. Wolinski and Sempé are eating at the next table over. They're two cartoonists with styles similar to mine, one with the *Hara-Kiri* group, the other with *L'Express*. Suddenly, I remember that I work for Wolinski's newspaper (he publishes my comics) and apologize profusely: I haven't drawn a thing in three months. He hadn't noticed, he says, but I really should get

9

back to work, I'm up to jack shit. I know. Where can I be found? Nowhere. I left my apartment, I haven't wanted to live there since Pierre died. There's an apartment for rent on my floor, Marielle tells me. I don't really feel like taking on a lease, I feel better in hotels, I go from one to the next, the first few days are always the best. I have three shirts, two pairs of jeans, two pairs of underwear, three or four pairs of socks, one sweater, a jacket, my toiletries, my notebook, and my Bic. It all fits in a big overnight bag or a small suitcase. I have some stuff at my dad's, but he doesn't even know I'm in Paris. Just get back to work, says Wolinski. It's the only way to get over it. He says he lost his wife and that it forced him to work, having to get by as a single dad with two daughters. Sempé also has two daughters. Marielle claims to have only brothers, as do I, the conversation bifurcates, Wolinski and Sempé talk about their daughters, we talk about our brothers. They have haddock, we have pot-au-feu. Marielle is even more beautiful than she was ten years ago, she has a sweeter laugh; she laughs inside her phrases and smiles inside mine. Sempé and Wolinski double over laughing every times the other says a line. They'll cool down with a cigar, drawing on the paper tablecloth. Marielle is writing a novel, too. She has hundreds of pages written, she'd like to get them in order. About Paris. Homosexuals? That's all just one neighborhood.

You're crazy, they're everywhere. We share a cigar, she has a cognac, I have a Calvados. It's true he was handsome, she says. One of the characters in her book is like him. A dumb, muscular queen. That's not like him at all, I argue. Marielle, like my editor, is confusing Pierre with someone else. Proust said it all, Sempé says. He was taking part in a completely different conversation. Marielle has to swing by the paper, I drop her off. And I find myself alone in a taxi, unsure of where to go. It's four in the afternoon. I go back to my hotel on Rue Bonaparte. I roll a cigarette with some Moroccan hash, I fall dead asleep. I wake up freezing cold at eight p.m., my mind made up. I pack my suitcase, hail a taxi, and go to a hotel on Boulevard Magenta. They take me for a bumpkin come to spend two weeks in Paris. Two weeks, that's a long time. To get by without sparing alcohol or marijuana, I've got the five thousand francs my editor gave me this afternoon. They give me a room with a bathroom overrun with cockroaches, a mattress full of lumps. A little black table, a chair, and a window overlooking the boulevard. An armchair I'll never use. I tell them I'm going to spend two weeks writing. I'm a writer. Although they find this suspicious at first (the hotel is run by a homely and penny pinching mother-daughter duo), after two or three days they get accustomed to my habits; I write for three or four hours on end, sleep for two or three, go out for a bite nearby, and come home to write. They're well aware that I'm in an altered state, but they don't care as long as I keep quiet and don't bring anyone back to my room. Only I have to hear the scratching of my Bic in my notebook, only I have to breathe in the smoke from my herb washed down generously with vodka. It's the only way I can build up the strength to kill Pierre. No one will come looking for me in this dreadful hotel. And if I feel like fucking on a break between two pages, there's no shortage of movie theater bathroom orgies just around the corner.

2

Confession

And you'll see from the start that this is a crime novel, that there are several crimes and two guilty parties, but no cops (I don't like that part of crime novels), and so, no punishments. For now, here's what I'm thinking for our first day of work together (since you'll be working with me to find pleasure whenever a crime takes place, I'm thinking of a strictly intellectual pleasure, naturally).

Here's my idea: in this book, I'll be a Masochist. I'll have gotten into it in 1965 once I started living publicly as a homosexual, after hiding it almost entirely for a long time. Masochism struck me as another homosexuality beyond homosexuality, an extra. Up to that point, I'd lived my sexuality as if it were a vice, but once it went public it practically became a virtue, so I sought shelter in Masochism. I had something like a dozen partners, a black guy from the States, a stripper girl, an old Surrealist painter. None of my friends, gay or straight, ever knew, and even as they read this now they'll probably think I'm just making things up, so pure a homosexual I seem to them. When I met Pierre in Rome, I had infected scars on my nipples, burns all over my ass, I'd come straight from Paris after a session that had gone overboard. Other people go see a psychoanalyst. In this sense, it cures me, I feel young and light-hearted. I'm gearing myself up for a perfect Roman vacation, I even agree to embody Romanticism, unavoidable in that old city, between two quick lays in a dark corner before going for a beer with my companion on Piazza Navona and lending him ten thousand liras which you'll never see again. When I came across Pierre I was completely blown away, all my senses transformed. He had no sexuality, none at all. He never got it up, didn't feel a thing, I could do whatever I wanted with him and, curiously enough, knowing full well that I could have wounded his manly Roman pride for my own entertainment, I chose to respect his evergreen summer body, tough where it was tan, soft where it was pale, which was Pietro himself, his entire being. What I loved about him most of all was his strong, ever-changing smell: that was his soul. Some people's dominant note wafts from their armpits, some from their feet, others from their sex, but Pietro's came from his hair, always the same, even after he washed it with shampoo. It smelled like the taste of honey, even though it was jet black and wiry. And braided in with that dominant note was an ever-changing pattern of a thousand combinations of aromas, that of his little feet, which lent a certain heft to his body's smell, that of his sex, which spoke to me like an antenna of the sexuality it detected around us, the jasmine aroma of his ever-moist balls, and his armpits, which infinitely mingled sour, sweet, and bitter notes according to his mood. Quickly I learn to interpret all these smells and use them to orient myself in the external world, they become my sixth sense. I can't stay away from Pietro. Whenever he's getting dressed, whenever he's cooking, whenever he's out for a walk, whenever he's taking a shower, whenever he's watching TV, I simply revolve around him to catch a whiff of his scent from up close. I've forbidden him any deodorant or cologne. He thinks I see him as a Roman masterpiece. A street kid, he's used to such tourism. Being more in love with me than he realizes, he needs my gaze to live, I'm already his killer. Well, perhaps killer is a strong word, I still don't know that I'm going to kill him, he doesn't know that I'm capable of forgetting him. So, I've already killed him as soon as I begin writing, the hypnotic back-and-forth of this Bic across my notebook blocks out the memory of his smell, I see that it must have been this constant motion of my eyes even when I'm not writing (I always write between three and fifteen hours a day) (even when I'm not writing, my eyes follow the movements of my Bic) that scared him away from me, twitchy like a reptile's, so distinct from the velvet eyes I tried to tame, to perforate. Ah, Pietro, I loved you for your gazelle-like gaze, too, your gaze that gasped for air whenever it received my barbs. I hurt you often, I know, and always so unfairly. I should have watched your life from afar, through binoculars, remained nothing more than a good friend. But I needed your smell as a target for my eyes—didn't you ever understand? No, you never understood. I frightened you, made you run away. You went off to seek shelter in a blonde woman's hollow regard and drowned in a lake of boiling steel. I should have left you in Rome and made a pilgrimage to come see you from time to time, the way people visit the Sistine Chapel. But it's too late, you've become Parisian, the very memory of Rome is unpleasant to you now, you steer clear of your fellow Latins who already seem too vulgar for you. You've traded in your blue jeans and Lacoste shirts for satin pants and Indian blouses, I gave you an amber and coral necklace that you wear out dancing at Leslie's, you go buy yourself your first dress at the flea market, I'll gift you Yves Saint Laurent's first platform shoes, you shave your legs, your chest, soon your beard, you adopt the afro hairstyle, you start taking feminine hormones. Your voice softens, little breasts crop up on your chest and I can't stop tonguing them, sucking them with adoration, I fuck your ass four times a day. Were we not happy? If not for your consuming obsession with becoming ever more of a woman. I see you again every day just as I saw you every morning back when we lived together, tweezers in hand, eyes staring deep into the magnifying mirror, plucking out the hairs of your Italian beard one by one, your face twisting with pain, on and on like this for hours until your cheeks are all bloody, and then you spend the whole afternoon icing them to make yourself presentable by evening under two smears of makeup and the dim light of a club. I can say that, during all those years, every time I wrote or drew I looked up from time to time at your martyrdom. What did I make of this martyrdom? Oh, I don't know. Was it for me you put yourself through all that? For my eyes? Can you imagine my confusion, my pain, when I find myself forced to write without you here beside me, when the only thing I see when I lift my eyes from the page is this sad little stretch of Boulevard Magenta? You're dead, and I can't write a word that's not about you. I miss you so much, I shut my notebook, roll a strong joint and smoke it, sobbing, finally I calm down, I take a shower. I'm completely insane for staying in this hotel that makes me so depressed, I should have gone to Morocco to write for a few weeks. But I've tried that one before, Morocco always makes me feel like drawing, never like writing. I decide to go to Marrakesh the next morning. Are there flights every day? Doesn't matter, I can always go to Tangiers. It's ten p.m., I haven't eaten all day, I should at least go out and have a sandwich. I've hardly written a word, Pietro's memory interrupts my sentences, I sit here with a pen or cigarette dangling from my fingers for minutes at a time, thinking about him. I walk out to the street drunk and stoned out of my mind, but I'm so used to it that the people around me don't even notice. I down a plate of steak frites and an undrinkable Bordeaux in a restaurant flooded with neon light. So as not to have to look at the people beside me, I start reading the *Paris-Match* photo captions. I'm not the only one here keeping to himself, people eat alone like they do in New York, the ones sitting together hardly speak, everybody's plunged in a tense stupor just like me. At least I have the excuse of being stoned. I have a good laugh, looking at the shots of Queen Juliana. I pay my tab, sipping a coffee with brandy at the bar. I make eyes at an Arab who's watching some French hoodlum play pinball. He looks back at me, we lock eyes, I flash him a smile, touching my fly. He starts touching his too, a grave look on his face. He's ugly and pretty old. I walk into the bathroom, you have to drop in a twenty-cent coin to open the toilet door. I've got one, I walk in, leaving the door ajar. The Arab shows up right away with an impenetrable attitude. He unbuttons his pants, I drop my briefs.

He has a long cock with a big head, I blow him. He takes me up the ass, but finishes immediately, I wipe myself off, he does too. Gallons of cum. He walks out without a smile, washes his hands. I'm completely turned on, I feel like dropping by the Tuileries. Out in the street, the thrill passes quickly. I go back to the hotel to write but fall asleep after giving my asshole a thorough cleansing, otherwise it's just one case of the clap after another. I wake up with a start like I always do when I'm writing, and roll myself a joint. I drink a fairly cold beer I'd left out on the windowsill. It's five a.m. All is quiet except for the sound of the odd car taking off with a green light. I read back over what I've written. I'm shocked to find that I haven't said a single word about Marilyn.

3

The Rival

Marilyn is a fag hag who styles her hair, makeup, and outfits completely after Marilyn Monroe, she imitates her every pout and gesture, the batting of the eyelashes, the heart-shaped mouth, it's all there. She owns replicas of Marilyn's dresses from her films and wears nothing else, flying in the face of current fashion. Naturally, she impersonates Marilyn Monroe down at the Alcazar, and for one summer she was every travesti's idol, but we met her mid-decline, replaced in her performance by an actual travesti with the exact same specialty. A star for her fifteen minutes, she took her fall poorly and tried to drown it out in screwdrivers at every queen bar where she still had a few acolytes. My poor Pierre was one of them. Almost every evening, she'd come by to pick us up for dinner at a restaurant where all the queens went, and then haul us around their clubs until five a.m. As soon as I noticed that Pierre was developing a naïve admiration for this foolish girl, I started to hate her, but I was very careful not to show her; I was jealous and I hid it well. And she adored Pierre. She stole him makeup and dresses from the boutiques. I never saw her spend a single sou, she stole everything. She lived in a hotel in Odéon, where she hadn't paid rent for two years, she sold her landlord the bags of weed that some old Colombian diplomat gave her in exchange for arranging an occasional orgy, but she made everyone pay to play, even the gigolos. She was always selling everyone everything and never buying anything herself. Once I watched her trade four ounces for a plane ticket to Río and flip that ticket for a house on Ibiza for a whole year in a matter of two phonecalls. At Le Pimm's, the club where she had been on top for a long time, nothing happened without her involvement, she'd rally everyone to go dancing at Le Petit-Vendôme, at sunrise she'd go smoke hash cigarettes in the Tuileries. She adored the queens and got them to accept her by acting like one of them. But she wasn't one of them at all. She fell all too violently in love with Pierre, she was the shrewdest opponent I've ever faced. And she won the first round by way of marriage. She and Pierre got married in 1967 in Amsterdam, she was dressed up as Marilyn Monroe, Pierre as Jane Russell in *Gentlemen Prefer Blondes*. To celebrate, she throws a party on a barge. I have to pay for all the drinks and drugs, and she panhandles for money after imitating Marilyn's "boop boop bee doop." She's already moved in with us on Boulevard Saint-Germain with enormous open trunks where the false dresses of Marilyn Monroe are on permanent display, she spends all day in the bathroom, plucking Pierre's hair all the way down to his ass while they gossip about whatever happened at Le Pimm's the night before. To get any writing done I have to take refuge in the kitchen, where neither of them ever sets foot, since she still hasn't thought to turn it into a solarium. She spends all day on the phone, sitting in Pierre's lap, plucking his hairs out with one hand and holding the phone with the other. She's making evening plans. On and on like this for hours. All the travestis have a landline at home. They tended to start turning up around eight, particularly the ones who didn't have bathrooms at home, each one with a bag of dresses and cosmetics, my apartment was the green room of a show that never made the stage, except in furtive outings to the clubs where other groups put on their shows. What were they living on? On Marilyn. They all sold small quantities of the hash that Marilyn supplied them with, stole their food in the supermarkets and their dresses in the Prisunic and the Marché aux Puces, some of them also had an older admirer who helped them out. They lent this money around internally without ever spending or investing a thing (or very infrequently), they amassed a small fortune this way and opened a bank account under Marilyn's legal name, Delphine Audieu. Even so, I was the one who paid the rent and the gas, electric, and phone bills, their drinks and the couscous they would order up from Place Maubert, their fines for public disturbances at night, and taxis, in exchange for which I gained access to hash cigarettes of the most dubious quality and their disdain. I spent my days barricaded off in the kitchen, sitting in front of the refrigerator, drawing nonstop to sustain this lifestyle. Now and then the door would fly open and Pierre would pass me a hash cigarette, squealing: Marilyn found me the most sublime dress! Do you think I'm pretty, darling? And he'd go spinning from the kitchen table to the fridge in a silver lamé miniskirt. I'd take him by the hand, trying to kiss his neck, and say: stay with me in the kitchen a while, let me smell your armpits. Oh, you monster, he'd cry, pushing me away. And with the booming guffaw of a Roman boy, he'd go back to the living room, from where their fits of crazy laughter, chitter-chatter, and clouds of hash smoke approached me. I leaned on the fridge, overwhelmed. Ever since Pierre had gotten married, he didn't let me touch or smell him. I was made to sleep on the other side of the bed, while Marilyn monitored us from a divan on the other side of the room. They all hated cock, Marilyn, still a virgin, most of all. And they weren't sleeping together, it never would have crossed their minds. All the bourgeois queen clubs had banned them, they were despised. They'd work the sidewalk on Rue Sainte-Anne, grab some drunk old man stumbling out of a bar, wrap themselves around him, Marilyn in her blue goat fur coat tell him about how she was a great star of the Alcazar to reassure him that his knickknacks wouldn't get stolen, and they'd invite him for a drink at La Pergola, then shoot him up with cocaine in the bathroom and walk him back to his house with his head spinning, terrified by the scandal his vice could cause to erupt in his family (even the loneliest old man has a distant niece, the family of an associate, or some manner of society among which a scandal can always break out). And what a spectacle it was! Completely different from the more refined sessions of my own Masochist days. They'd tie the old man down to the bed with sheets, piss and shit on him and spit in his eyes, whipping him with a wet towel. Marilyn always carried a little battery with two electrodes in her purse, they'd stick one right up the old man's ass and put the other in his mouth, they'd make contact and the antique would start shrieking despite the electrode in his mouth, writhing around, they'd redouble their whipping and start clawing him. By the time they turned the thing off, the guy would be lying there passed out, they'd howl like Indians, ransacking the apartment, we'd all scatter in radio-taxis and no one ever filed a single police report. I saw them do this on Avenue Foch, in Parc Monceau and Place de l'Alma. And as soon as the old man got back on his feet after his little adventure and showed his face again on Saint-Anne, the travestis would harangue him, pushing him around, stealing his hat, pinching his asscheeks. And so he'd walk into Le Sept with tousled hair, a crooked tie, a red face, and watery eyes. The other old rich queens would hardly even greet him, an exile from his society, fallen to the rung of the Masochists. Poor thing, after two hours in the bar amidst the total indifference of his peers, he would find himself once again on the sidewalk surrounded by Marilyn's gang, who, this time, extorted signed blank checks from him without even needing to touch him. How could I have put up with this life for ten years, why did I cut myself off from my leftist friends, from Marielle de Lesseps, from my editor, to become a silent witness to this revolting merry-go-round? Because I loved Pierre. Pierre, whom I knew I'd lose forever if I let him out of my sight for a single minute, not because he'd leave me (now I know he'll never leave me), but because if I go back to my friends (who, for that matter, can't stand him), I run the risk of going astray toward a different sensibility, myself. I give him all my attention, even my workdays. I remember drawing day and night for an entire month just to buy him a monkey fur coat. And maybe I also had the premonition that he was going to die young, I didn't want to miss a single second of his life. But I would have liked a bit more peace and quiet, I was far from sharing in that hysteria common among the groups of travestis, they fight over hand-kerchiefs and break each other's noses over a john (do they not go so far as to kill?). They all carry switchblades in their purses because, they say, people attack them in the streets. Some of them ride motorcycles and wear black leather, they go out looking for the old Masochists who cruise the Bois de Boulogne in their cars, flagellating them with bike chains for five hundred francs a pop (and I'm talking new francs). Soon they're rich enough to invest (their society has something like thirty members) in a print shop where they produce a porno mag all on their own. And so I saw my apart-ment converted into a photo studio, there were machines all over the place that consumed enor-mous amounts of electricity at my expense, my kitchen into a darkroom, I found myself forced to take refuge and write in the bathroom, which also served as the dressing room where they put on makeup, lubed up their assholes, put on their cock rings, touching themselves nonstop to get hard, since the feminine hormones they downed by the fistful made keeping an erection difficult. As soon as one of them is hard, Marilyn rushes over to focus the camera, another one flashes her asshole, the others move around with the spotlights and props (pelts, feathers, pearls, dildos, whips, stilettos), the makeup artist hastily powders the model's breasts, legs, balls in a flurry of nerves, she doesn't want the model to lose it before everything's ready for the photo. To prevent this, someone gives the model a blowjob. Marilyn adjusts the lighting on one's leather pants, on another's bare ass, adjusts the angle of a spotlight, or quickly adds in a pair of sequin suspenders, a green feather boa, or a satin pillow. Their magazine is prohibited from public display but sells for its weight in gold at the queen clubs. They even get invited to Chez Régine, where they steal a mink coat and rough up the bouncer. And Marilyn reigns over that whole world. She decides to become a director, they've earned enough money to make a film. I shudder at the thought of her asking me to write the script. But no, Pierre's her screenwriter! This perfidious girl has found a way to hit Pierre in his creativity, which, as is the case with any Roman, is bound up with his manhood. She pushes him to find a subject for the movie in his childhood, Pierre's terrified of film because it reminds him of his parents' death, but she convinces him he needs to do away with that fear, it's his duty. My poor Pierre comes up with ideas that are impossible for the team of actors: he draws inspiration from the Cinecittà fire that killed his father, he imagines a picture à la Cecil B. DeMille, only set against a humanitarian backdrop, a bit like *The Towering Inferno*, in which all the characters would have been players dressed up to meet the needs of the film they were shooting, we would have seen Cleopatra, Scarlet O'Hara, Ben-Hur, Nero, Buffalo Bill, and hundreds of elephants, horses, and stagehands go up in the blaze. Perfectly unrealizable, given the budget of the group, which in any event has no interest in departing from strictly erotic content. The movie project gets shelved. But something's stuck in Pierre's mind, I can tell, he looks distracted, he's less flirtatious, I wake up at night and catch him lying there beside me with his big eyes wide open, it's the first time something like that has happened. I reach out and touch his back, he pulls away bereft of affection, Marilyn snores on the couch. I get up, get dressed in silence, he doesn't look away from the ceiling lit by streetlight. I go out to the street, cross the Île Saint-Louis, and have a drink at La Mendigotte where there's hardly a soul left. I toss back four whiskeys, slouched over on my stool in the deafening music. Completely wasted, I decide to leave Pierre. Wasn't he the one who left me first? I stumble home in zigzags (ID check on the Pont Marie), it's six a.m. in winter, the apartment is quiet, it's not cold, I'm sleepy, I fix myself up a cup of Viandox in what's left of my kitchen between the photo-enlargers, I decide to lie down and have a serious conversation with Pierre the next day. I tiptoe into the bedroom and hear two people panting on the creaking bed. My jealousy reaches fever pitch, blood rushes to my head. I turn on the light. What's wrong? says Pierre, while still fucking Marilyn in the ass. I'm leaving, I say. Where are you going? Pierre asks me after a pause. Rome! I tell him. I start packing my suitcase. Why? asks Pierre. And after a moment: You don't love me anymore? No, I say, I don't love you anymore. I was crying as I threw my clothes haphazardly into my suitcase, I called a cab. I'll take the first flight out to Rome. Pierre gets up, slips on a diaphanous dressing gown. But what's wrong? he asks. Nothing, I tell him, sobbing, absolutely nothing. I take my suitcase and slam the door on my way out of the apartment. Pierre grabs me in the hallway. But what's wrong? he repeats. Are you mad because I was with Marilyn? I swear I won't do it again. I take advantage of his promise, and ask for more: I never want to see her again! The taxi driver opens the trunk. He seems curious about the little breasts Pierre is flashing through his robe in the middle of winter. But what has she ever done to you? Pierre asks. What's so wrong with us sleeping together? Nothing, actually, but when I get back I want her gone with her travestis and all their machines (there's video equipment now, too), I'll be back in a week! I shut the taxi door and we take off. The thought that I could find another guy like him in Rome has got to make him jealous. And I'm hell-bent on finding one, I want revenge. I'll come back with an even younger and more handsome Roman who fucks me right and leaves me in peace. And I'll throw all those girls out on their asses, starting with Marilyn. Was that a guy? the taxi driver asks. Yep. Er, he's got some amazing tits. Tits can grow if you want them to, I snap back in a huff, you could have some too. You really think so? Me? he says, and starts laughing. It's such a drag, spending the whole day as a target for comments like this from everyone, on the street, in public places. In fact, I think that Pierre and the rest of them are really courageous. Personally, I'm not a travesti because I'm not brave enough. For a second I consider getting a sex change, I think it's the only way to get Pierre back. I think about my skinny little body, my big pointy nose. Maybe if I'd done it when I was younger. Everyone I know who's gotten a sex change did it too late, in the US they hop right to it when they turn eighteen, the legal age, and it's already too late. They should let people get sex changes around puberty, before the masculine features really start to accentuate. How many twelve year old boys would choose to be girls if it weren't for the nightmarish world of clinics? Would I have dared when I was twelve, when I felt more like a girl than ever? I'm almost convinced of it, but back then no one even considered the problem, I wasn't even aware of the possibility. It will be ten years before there are any convincing travestis in France. I heard tell of one in New York who, at twenty-five, married a Protestant preacher who didn't suspect a thing, and they adopted a little Asian kid together. And I don't doubt it, given the advances the Americans have made in this field, but it's crucial, I'll say it again, to make up your mind early. Pierre was too old when he got into it, the peskiest parts were his beard and Adam's apple, to say nothing of his arched legs, his muscular arms, and his chest hair, which for the most part still lingered on his breasts, two balls filled with paraffin, which he now shaved, having grown tired of those sessions of electric hair removal, so painful for him and so expensive for me. Sometimes I felt like I was holding two enormous testicles in my hands and that idea turned me on even more, with its dash of surrealism. At the same time, he started getting extremely turned on whenever I licked his bellybutton. His bellybutton was deep and smelled faintly of ass. It wasn't long before I was able to stick two fingers into it, then my entire cock. His spasms were constant, insane, as were mine, I felt like I was penetrating Pierre more deeply than any other asshole or pussy in the world could have been penetrated. He referred to the orgasms I gave him as "Gioia Divina," a phrase he'd cry out every time I stuck my cock into his bellybutton while suckling and nibbling his huge testicle breasts. I've never heard of another bellybutton like his, it must have been a sort of oddity of nature. Was it the hormones? I doubt it, although he had been taking them for a year when I discovered this new erogenous zone, which for that matter quickly turned into our central, almost unique focus in sex. Pierre recalled fondling his bellybutton when he was younger, but no more than his asshole, never his cock. His belly-button had always been deeper than normal, and when he was very young he kept the coins he fished out of the Fontana de Trevi in it, while the other kids kept them in their mouths. But he never paid much attention to it, I was the one who took its virginity. I made him swear to me that he'd never share it with anyone else, I was horrified to think that he might someday get used to a cock bigger than mine, whenever he left the house I made him wear a Band-Aid over his bellybutton, which I always checked as soon as he came home, and I never let him go out alone at night, either. I should say, to his Roman honor, that nobody but me ever knew his bellybutton, maybe because he was ashamed of it. How is it possible that Marilyn, that idiot, never suspected anything? And besides, how was she getting him hard? Suddenly, I sit bolt upright in the taxi, cracking her whole scheme just as we pull up to Orly. I drop off my suitcase with a porter and run to the nearest payphone, I call my apartment, the line's busy. She's been switching out Pierre's feminine hormones for masculine ones in the pill bottle he always carries in his bag! And she's been doing it for some time now, since the marriage, to be exact. My line is still busy, as always, as soon as the moment the first travesti hops out of bed. I hail another taxi and in my excitement almost forget my suitcase with the porter I dropped it off with. I'm running late, I tell the taxi driver, I'll give you a nice tip if we make it quick to Boulevard Saint-Germain. Number 2! Ah, that's gonna be tough, the taxi driver says. And he drives back to the city leisurely, racking up traffic jams. My irritation has evolved into a cold anger, the anger of a judge. Switching out someone's hormone pills seems like a crime against human identity. As if there weren't enough normal men in the world already! The taxi driver stops at a red light. I realize it's the same guy who picked me up a few minutes ago. Did you forget something? he asks me. My passport, I tell him. Where are you going? Rome. Do you like guys? I actually look at him for the first time. He's handsome, nothing to write home about. Redhead. Curly hair, wide smile. Twenty-five, I'd guess, though one can never tell. The car starts again with the green light. What about you? I ask him. He smiles in the rear-view mirror. I'm Moroccan. But you're a redhead. It's henna! He lights a cigarette. What part are you from? It's complicated:

he was born in Ketama and grew up between Tangiers, Casablanca, and Agadir. And what are you up to here? Driving this taxi. He laughs, takes off again when the light turns green. I only know Marrakesh, I tell him. Some real pretty boys there, he says and laughs. He has a gold tooth. He stares into my eyes, I'm forced to smile. He notices right away that I have a rotten tooth, monitoring Pierre's comings and goings so closely I haven't even had time to go to the dentist. We get stuck in another traffic jam. I don't know what to say: Well, winter in Paris sure isn't the same as in Morocco. He laughs. Do you live alone? he asks. He knows perfectly well that I don't, he saw Pierre this morning and overheard our conversation. No, I answer sharply. It's the kind of come-on that gets on my nerves. Ever since I've been surrounded by trannies everyone thinks I'm either a bottom or a pimp, or both. And worst of all are my leftist friends, who take me for a victim of society (the society of queens, of course), although I do share that opinion from time to time. We arrive, I hand him a fifty franc bill and run up the stairs two by two. Nobody's home. There's a letter in Pierre's round, childish handwriting on my recently made bed (they cleaned the house before leaving). I can tell straight away from the tone and grammar that Marilyn dictated it: "We want to live a normal life as a couple. Thank you for everything you have given me. Yours, Pierre." My disdain for that woman made me underestimate her. But where'd they go? Someone buzzes at the door. It's the taxi driver with my suitcase, I'd forgotten it in his trunk. He's gone? he asks, seeing me with the letter in my hand. And he walks in without putting down the suitcase. He looks around the living room and says: Nice place. I close the door. Stay for a beer, I tell him. The taximeter's running, he says. I'll pay it. He doesn't drink on the job. I've got some hash. That sounds good, a little toke. He smokes and looks at the trannies' clothes hanging on a rack. You're the one who wears this stuff? he asks. No, never. Let me see how it looks on you. I undress in the bathroom and put on a silver sequin dress that's too big for me. I notice him standing in the door-way, he's been watching me. Do you like it? I ask. He comes up to me and grabs my ass, a cigarette dangling from his lips. His leather jacket gives off a strong smell, so does he. He turns me around, unbuttoning his pants, tells me to unzip mine. The phone rings. Hold on a sec, I tell him. It's Pierre. In a solemn voice, he tells me: I've thought it over. I'm leaving Marilyn Monroe (why Monroe? We never called her Monroe). Silence. Alright, I say, come home, then. I don't have cash for the taxi, he tells me. That vile girl stranded him at Charles de Gaulle and hopped alone on a plane to Ibiza. The taxi driver is behind me, trying to pry my asscheeks apart. I push him away with my elbow. I'll pay your fare, I tell Pierre. And after a pause, he asks me: Do you forgive me? Of course I forgive him. Can we rebuild life together? The candor of this clumsy question moves me, I have a knot in my throat. I'm just barely able to say, "yes, I love you," and hang up, sobbing. The taxi driver seems especially turned on now, he rips open the stitching that follows my fly, grunts, trying to push his cock into my asshole, which I squeeze tight. The more his head hurts, the more it excites him, he thrusts against me without pulling out at all, until I let him in all at once. He gasps, and just like that he's finished. It's always the same with these Arab guys. Without saying a thing, he washes up, soaps off his cock without daring to look at me in the mirror he's facing. Did you like it? I ask him, leaning on the doorframe. I see myself perfectly in the mirror, my long hair is a complete mess, my dress is torn, like a freshly raped prostitute. The taxi drivers laughs and looks embarrassed. I've got to get back to it, he says. I have to give my boss a hundred francs by noon. Only a hundred francs! To think there are queens afraid to walk the street and get robbed or killed by some gigolo they've picked up at the club! Come back whenever you want, I tell him. You can sleep with my friend too, if you want to. I try to get him hard again, he pushes me away nicely and says: I'm married. I take a hundred franc note out of the pocket of my pants on the floor. Don't want to cheat on your wife? I ask him. No, he has two kids. They look like him. They play soccer. He buttons back up, I walk out with him to the landing, I'm giving him a kiss on both cheeks right when the old lady from upstairs walks by with her shopping basket. The taximeter's running, he offers as an excuse, and walks down. Pierre bolts past him at full speed up the stairs, and says: Give me a hundred francs! I run to the bathroom and grab another hundred franc note from my pocket. My neighbor howls on the landing: I'll tell the landlord! I hand Pierre the hundred francs and he runs down to pay for the second taxi. The woman writes to the landlord every time she sees a man dressed like a woman on the stairs, and to that purpose she wears herself out walking up and down them all day long. Her obsession is so far-reaching that she believes that even my grandmother, who dropped by one day to see me, is a crossdresser, too. And each of her letters gives my landlord another excuse to raise my rent. Pulling up the plunging neckline of my dress, I ask her, How are your cats, Madame Choyeuse? (I'm not kidding, her last name means "Coddler.") My cats? My cats? What do you care about my cats? And she whips a leek out of her basket and starts smacking me with it. I try to hold her at bay, but she only hits me harder, meowing. Leek leaves scatter all over the landing. Pierre comes up the stairs, shrieking like a true queen, and comes to my rescue.

You crazy hag! he screams at Madame Choyeuse. Leave my poor Raoul alone! I'm his poor Raoul (that's my real name, my name is Raoul Damonte but I sign my books as Copi because that's what my mom has always called me, I don't know why). Then he pushes me inside and slams the door shut. Did she hurt you? he asks me with exaggerated concern, holding my shoulders. No! No! I shake it off. He kisses my mouth, which is to say he sucks and bites my lips without letting go of them for a good two minutes, as Italians tend to do, I feel his tears streaming down my nose. He falls to his knees, kissing the edge of my skirt, clasping my hands: I swear to you, I'll never sleep with another woman! I free up a hand to stroke his hair. And that's when the miracle happens: his frizzy hair electrifies the lines of my finger, I get goosebumps. Pietro, Pietro! I whisper, falling to my knees and licking his tears, his neck, his breasts, he slips his hand under my skirt and, with his index finger, strokes my anus flooded with the taxi driver's cum. Pietro, Pietro, I sob, undoing his belt, licking his bellybutton. He screams: Amore! amore! And I notice he's gotten hard! His cock, which has never been any bigger than a string bean, is stiff and erect. The masculine hormones have dictated their laws. I lie him down on his back, lifting my skirt, and I sit on his cock, which tickles my asshole with that gentleness defin-itive of Pierre's entire charm, his elegance. Together forever, he whispers, sempre insieme! Sempre, sempre, sempre! I sob, cumming. My sperm rains down upon his hairy torso, I use it as lubricant on his bellybutton, sticking three fingers in, and he shouts in his baritone, vengo! vengo! And he cums, at last, I feel his little cock stirring around inside me like a teaspoon in a cup of coffee, while I move multiple fingers inside his bellybutton, it's like a mucous membrane corkscrew, I push my entire hand inside, my bicep begins to spasm and, for the first time in my life, my right arm has an orgasm. In his belly, my hand is like a fish in water, he contorts, screaming, Miracolo! Miracolo! then collapses, bloodless, pale, hardly breathing, a strand of drool falling from the corner of his mouth. I púll my hand out gently, wipe the sweat-soaked hair off his forehead, and whisper, "I love you." I squeeze myself against him, sticking my nose into his armpit, he puts his arms around me, we both fall asleep on the floor.

4

New York Snake

Someone's knocking. I wonder where I am. In a hotel on Boulevard Magenta, 7 a.m. The landlady's daughter asks if I plan to keep the room. They find me more suspicious every day. I'm stoned and dead drunk. Yes, I'm staying, I ask her to send up breakfast, one large café au lait and two croissants. This gesture of authority puts her at ease, she sets the tray down on the little black table next to my notebook, I take a shower, and shout from the bathroom: I was working all night! I come out wearing a towel, she's reading my notebook. Do you work for a magazine? she asks. I work for a publishing house, not the papers. Should she clean my room? I'll make the bed myself, thanks. That way she'll leave me alone all day. I give her a twenty franc tip, wolf down my breakfast, and fall back asleep. At noon, someone's knocking on my door. A woman died in the room next door last night. Did I hear anything? Nothing at all. She hanged herself. A cop takes notes. I didn't go out last night, just an hour for dinner, I fell asleep and wrote and I didn't hear anything except the cars taking off at the green light. She hanged herself around six a.m., I was alone, I was writing, and even so I didn't hear even the slightest sound, she hanged herself in the shower, kicking over a stool, then spent a long time dying and thrashing around so much she even broke the sink and the mirror. I didn't hear a thing. And yet her bathroom window opens right onto mine. And both were open. From where I was writing, I could have seen her if I turned around. I never even realized my bathroom had a window. Your papers, says the cop. He checks them over a hundred times. Meanwhile, they cart the body out into the hallway on a stretcher draped in a sheet, it's so narrow that they have to carry her out upright. The sheet slides off, uncovering Marilyn's bloated face. I scream and wake up in a cold sweat. My head is pounding: I hardly ate a thing yesterday, didn't get enough sleep, and spent the whole day drinking vodka and smoking weed, both of which I always keep within reach. I'll have to eat and sleep well today or I'll get sick, it wouldn't be the first time I've been forced to check in for a detox when I make it to the last page of a notebook. I must be tripping, I tell myself. Just another braindead hippie. And at my age! I take a shower, walk downstairs. I didn't realize you were in your room, the landlady says to me. Have you seen the papers? Marilyn Monroe died. Poor girl!

But she's been dead for at least a decade, I tell her. She shows me the front page of *Ici-Paris*: a Marilyn Monroe impersonator has hanged herself in her cell at the Regina Coeli Prison in Rome: it's Marilyn, my Marilyn! They'd hit her with twenty years for selling heroin! I'm speechless. I saw her at the Alcazar, the landlady tells me. She was really cute. Well, I'm off to lunch, I say, and walk out to Boulevard Magenta, bowled over by the news. So, she'd started selling heroin since the last time I saw her six months ago! Or maybe she was already involved by then. Poor Marilyn! I should mention that I've hardly seen her these past few years. Ever since I managed to triumph over her in Pierre's heart, she'd sunk, to forget him, into a hetero trip of the most sinister kind: she'd gotten herself a room in New York at the Chelsea Hotel and was trying her hand at underground film. To help herself along, she'd changed her style: nobody wanted Marilyns anymore, so she'd become a Garbo, even if she was a little too old for it. Pierre and I took a trip to New York in the spring of 1974, she'd let us know she didn't hang out with queens anymore, now it was Puerto Ricans and film directors. By this time, Pierre and I, having meanwhile become thirty-somethings with short slicked-back hair and sharp clothes from Cerutti, really appreciate each other now and hardly ever make love, but we're extremely sociable, and we hope to find in

Marilyn, in that New York of demented and frightening queens, a link to our past, let's say. Marilyn-Garbo is inscrutable. Plus, she makes us call her Greta. She greets us in a black dress woven with human hair. She doesn't realize that she looks more like Juliette Gréco than Greta Garbo. She sucks down one hash cigarette after another through a cigarette-holder as black as her wig, if it weren't for her red clogs, you might think she was just one great wig from head to toe. She's gotten so thin. Hello, she says, kissing Pierre and me each on one cheek. I have superb cocaine! We walk into her big hotel room, which she's wallpapered almost entirely in shiny yellow plastic. She's painted the windows a sky blue, there are tons of plants, and air conditioning. She asks us to take off our shoes and leave them by the door. She lives in terror of pollution. She doesn't drink anymore and follows a macrobiotic diet, she hands us two cups of lemon juice with yogurt and two pieces of ginger cake. She has a greenish boa constrictor named Dédé (short for Désirée), which she strokes, wraps in Indian headscarves, treats like a pet cat. The boa takes an interest in one of the suede moccasins that Pierre left by the door, stares at it and then licks it with its forked tongue, Pierre looks worried. She is not bad, she is only interested on your shoe, Marilyn-Garbo says in English with an accent like Maurice Chevalier. The boa bites the shoe and twists around.

Marilyn laughs a cold, American laugh. I love Dédé, she says, she is so incredible! The boa lifts the moccasin up into the air, slithers through the bathroom door. Marilyn screams. The boa drops it into the toilet bowl. Pierre's moccasin is completely soaked and Marilyn yells at the boa: You are terrible! Go back to the fridge! The boa lives in the refrigerator alongside a saucisson sec that someone brought her from Paris a few months ago: Marilyn hasn't eaten meat since she went macrobiotic. She keeps the sausage around for anyone who might want it, but all her friends are macrobiotic, too. We don't want any, either. She opens the oven door and takes out a Chinese bowl filled with cocaine, which we hit off a teaspoon. New York is fantastic! she says. You are always high! We try to bring up some memories: Boulevard Saint-Germain, Le Fiacre. Paris is horrible! she says, her eyes bugging out. So provincial! Pierre and I feel self-conscious, so out of the loop. Our form-fitting clothes, which we'd bought specially for New York at Cerruti in Paris, are uncomfortable, everyone here works a loose, disheveled style. We landed in New York in a state of euphoria, but we checked out every queen club and no one so much as looked at us, Pierre and I must seem like Pierre Cardin's twin brothers. But Marilyn doesn't want to hand over New York's secret to us, as she gave Pierre Paris's back in '65, she snubs us. Her love for Pierre has existed by way of hatred, now she hardly even notices him anymore. She asks what we're doing in town. We are in holidays, Pierre says in his funny English. And who do we see in Paris these days? Nobody, or hardly anyone. Pierre's started working with Dior, cutting dresses. I'm still drawing comics for the papers, I've written and staged a few plays. How's La Coupole? she asks. We never go to La Coupole, we hardly go out, we work, we watch TV. I see a flash of glee in that idiotic girl's eye: she thinks we're all settled down in a boring marriage. As if TV weren't more entertaining than a boa constrictor in a fridge! Not knowing what to talk about, she turns on the TV. It's a cartoon, a spider gobbling up a little Tarzan. I love freak's movies, she says, still insisting on speaking in her twisted English. There's nothing on but montages of insects, amphibians, and reptiles eating tiny human heroes. The boa emerges from the fridge and slithers over to eat the ginger cake crumbs on the purple carpet in front of the color TV set. Marilyn's agent calls: come tonight at midnight with your boa to the top of the Empire State Building for an apple juice commercial, she discusses the possibility of royalties for the boa; they're not on the table for the snake, she's furious. She kicks us out, she has to run to the acupuncturist's so she can get rid of these bags under her eyes before filming the commercial, the boa needs its acupuncture session, too, if not, it could get anxious and bite the camera man. She leaves us in the Chelsea Hotel hallway, Pierre holding his soaking moccasin, says see you later, and shuts the door. That's when Pierre drops the bomb with a simple phrase: I'm still in love with Marilyn. I don't get it. This isn't even the same girl, she's lost all her charm, she just looks like an old tranny. Pierre slaps me across the face. He rings Marilyn's bell, Marilyn opens up, throws herself into his arms, and they stand there hugging each other for a long time. Go back to Paris, you fuck, you faggot! Marilyn screams in my face. They walk into her room and close the door. If we'd been in Paris I would have made a scene, I'd have broken the door down. But in this enormous hotel hallway in New York I feel out of sorts, hesitant. Oh well, I'll wait. I rent a room on the same hallway, spend my days spying on their comings and goings through a little peephole I get specially installed in the middle of my door. They go out a lot, Marilyn bought him a tweed jacket and a red velvet cap, and she wears a new dress every night, always with that greenish piece of shit boa constrictor over her shoulders. Pierre found a job through some Italian relative on his father's side, a Gentiluomo mafioso who opened a club for Puerto Rican queens in Greenwich village. Pierre strips there, the audience stuffs fifty dollar bills into his bellybutton while he belly dances. Marilyn is also belly dancing in a Japanese lesbian club right next

47

door, when their shifts end they meet on the sidewalk in front of their respective clubs and go eat burgers together at Max's Kansas City while the boa snoozes under the table. I sit at a table nearby and watch them. My presence bothers them, but they're so intent on pretending they can't see me that they're forced into coming to eat always at the same restaurant and the same table, I've been set up at the facing table since around eight p.m., reading French papers, and biding my time. I'm wearing dark glasses, a blue silk scarf. I watch them from behind my glasses, pretending to read *Le Monde*. They're both wearing white raincoats, which they never take off, not even at the table, they both have the same pixie haircut, they kiss each other on the lips between bites of their burgers, they gaze into each other's eyes, sad, tired from their night's work. They put aside money to buy a farm on Ibiza that costs next to nothing, they add on a room for the kids, he plants tomatoes while she takes care of the little ones, it's bliss. They eat with one hand and cling to each other with the other. My poor Pierre looks so thin. He disdains me now as an honest family man disdains a john. When they get up from the table, she tosses her dozing boa constrictor around her neck while Pierre pays at the register. I'm sitting right there, he pretends not to see the tears falling behind my sunglasses. Pierre, I murmur, Pietro… As soon as they've given him his change, he looks right at me, and tells me off: When are you going to stop following me, you dirty faggot? And Marilyn screams at me: Fuck you! Fuck you! And they walk out of the restaurant, arm in arm. The cashier is used to this kind of scene, she watches me cry every night at closing time. Then I walk back to the hotel, depressed, I don't even feel like cruising. I know that Pierre will return to me someday, but when? One fine day, he walks across the hallway, knocks on my door. I open up. I'm back, he says. He kisses me on both cheeks. I cry, throwing myself around his neck. Oh, don't be so sentimental! he says, pushing me away. We're too old for that! Let's get back together, but on one condition: we can't touch anymore. The boa constrictor tried to strangle him in the night, he asked Marilyn to get rid of it, but she chose the boa over Pierre, and now he feels repulsed by the thought of being touched by any living creature. He wants to leave the States. He used the money he saved up as a stripper girl to buy me a little ruby, and he hands it to me as a gift. Then he collapses, kissing my hands, tells me that if he abandoned me, the city's to blame (se la città è fredda io sono freddo), that, deep down, I'm the one he really loves. But I'm getting a little tired of this. I didn't imagine his return would be like this, so formal. Maybe we played our roles too enthusiastically and after five years together we have gotten bored, monotonous, sucked dry of imagination. Someone knocks on the door. It's the boa, banging its head against the wood. It's carrying a letter in its mouth, addressed to me. I say thanks and close the door. I tear open the envelope. Pierre reads over my shoulder: "Here, have Pierre back. But watch out, he has syphilis." Something inside me snaps under this newfound depravity. I run across the hall, knock on Marilyn's door. The door opens and I see her in a black slip, her hair's a total mess, her eyes bloodshot with tears, shaking like a leaf from all the coke she's just blown. It's your turn to cry now, you slut! I tell her. And I slap her across the face. She leaps on top of me like a hyena, clawing at my face, we're tangled up in blows, I grab her throat, Pierre pulls us apart with the help of a bellhop who came running when he heard the commotion, the bellhop holds my arms behind my back while Pierre restrains Marilyn. I feel an unbearable pain in my calf, the boa's biting me, I scream, the boa won't let go, Pierre tries to yank on the snake's tail but it's slippery, the bellhop pulls me in the opposite direction. Marilyn takes this opportunity to hit me over the head with a huge glass ashtray. Finally, the bellhop runs to the kitchen for a knife, sticks it into the boa's mouth and tries to pry its jaws apart, I feel like I'm going to faint from the pain. The bellhop's quick on his feet, as soon as he can tell that the boa isn't going to give up its prey so easily, he sinks the knife in between two vertebrae just beneath its skull. The boa's eyes go murky, it groans but it won't let go. Marilyn starts shrieking, tries to stop him from stabbing the boa's neck again, but he fights her off with a cross to the jaw I would have savored under any other circumstances. He removes the knife from the snake's spine and then decapitates it, the boa's head is severed but it still won't let go. Its headless body thrashes around like a spring, a fountain of cold blood shoots out of its neck, spraying all over the screaming neighbors who came out of their rooms, I'm drenched. Pierre ran off to call an ambulance, it's already here. I have cold sweats, my teeth are chattering, the cramps in my foot and calf are increasingly painful. All four enormous fangs have pierced clear through my leg between the tibia and fibula, I'm fastened to the head of this snake whose dead dog eyes frighten me more and more, I faint in the ambulance. Pierre is next to me, holding my hand and praying in Italian while I fade from consciousness. I wake up on an operating table, a crowd of people bustling around me, they've cut off my pant leg and my leg is massive and violet, someone's removing the snake's head with an electric saw, which has me screaming in pain, they stick a rag soaked in ether over my nose, I watch the bright surgical lights dance around me, the snake's terrifying gaze reflected in every one of them, and fall unconscious again. When I wake up my head is spinning and I'm in excruciating pain, I look around. It's almost completely dark, I'm in a perfectly white, super-sterilized hospital room, Pierre's sleeping in his clothes on the bed beside me. I try to move in bed but feel a sharp pain in my left foot. I lift the sheets: there's no left foot there anymore. My leg ends at the knee in an immaculate and handsome white bandage. I'm dressed in nylon pajamas with the American flag on them (we're in style for the upcoming bicentennial), the left pant leg of which was cut at the thigh to leave this monstrosity on full display. I start weeping. Pierre wakes up, holds me in his arms, we cry together for a long time. Marilyn is waiting out in the hall to apologize. I refuse to see her. The operation went fine, they separated the bones like a chicken's, I was lucky because a major American specialist happened to be at the clinic when I arrived, ten minutes more and the gangrene would have consumed my entire leg. There's no effective antidote against that species of reptile, it's the product of a recent crossbreeding, in fact it's not even a true boa constrictor, it's closer to a python. They left me its head as a souvenir. The rectangular skull, cut in two, nice and clean in a jar of formaldehyde. And my leg? It's in a freezer, they're waiting for my decision. Pierre says we should bury it in the little cemetery in Marinella where his mom and dad are buried, it won't take up too much space, they'll bury it in a coffin for a child. Then when I die completely, they'll just toss it into my normal-sized coffin. It seems ridiculous to me. I'd rather they just throw it out. That's forbidden. Pierre doesn't want them to cremate it (never!), he insists, the leg flies alone to Rome where it's buried after a mass (they all think it's one of their grandchildren) by Pierre's maternal grandparents, extremely pious people from Trastevere who spend half their time kneeling in prayer in front of the Vatican. We decide to spend the winter on Ibiza, thankfully it wasn't my arm they cut off, I'll rest up and draw for the French and Italian papers while getting used to my light metal prosthesis, so painful for the first few months. They let me out of the hospital after three weeks, I have a monstrous stump that will slowly scar over until it's covered in hypersensitive pink skin like the head of a penis, I slather it with antibiotic ointment.

5

Ibiza

We rent a little house by the sea, see very few people, I smoke hash like a madman and sit in my wheelchair all day drawing comics on the patio, Pierre does all our shopping, he's spoiling me; I've become extremely capricious, I never let him go out, he spends his days cleaning and cooking meals for me with plenty of bay leaf. It's off-season, there's only one movie theater open and it plays completely asinine Argentine films. We bought a Citroën 2CV with no back seat to transport the gas tanks we use to heat the house. Our house is as ugly as all the others here, whitewashed, with windows shaped like kidneys, same as the pool, which is always coated with dead leaves and mosquitos, two rats drowned in it, we had to hire a company to come switch out the water, they'd hardly changed it before it was good for nothing again. Plus, it was right in the middle of all the rooms, there was no way to escape its fetid smell. Anyway, I'll be telling you more about this pool again later. Two or three times a week we go have an aperitif on the port with a group of old hippies who own shops that sell moccasins and Indian belts they make through the winter and sell to tourists in the summer. Now and then we sleep with a rather thickset guy (Michael) from their group, who likes one thing and one thing only, which is having his dick bitten, it's small and forked, but we put up with him because he gives us acid, which Pierre loves and which is hard to find on Ibiza in the winter. He lives alone with a wolf some three-hundred yards from our house in the ruins of a bread oven, he receives a monthly allowance of one-hundred forty dollars in stocks in an electric nutcracker company from a dead American aunt, which he spends on acid. Back in the day he took part in happenings, sometimes he still puts them on in his friends' shops, rolling on the ground and screaming, he slits a chicken's throat and sprays us all with its blood. The ten or fifteen hippies in the audience are into it, he asks for money, we all go out for shrimp in a bug-ridden hole that stinks of fried food and rotten fish, everyone pays his own part of the check. He's from the States, his full name is Michael Buonarrotti, he knows a few phrases in Italian, a handful more in American English, and not a word of any other language. He became a deaf-mute as a baby because he fell out of his crib and right onto his head, it broke his nose like a boxer's for good, his hair is red and frizzy.

He breathes fire at the table, the other braindead hippies get a kick out of it. All the same, he and I share a certain invalid's sympathy for one another, he hands me my cane when I get up from the table to go to the bathroom, I shout into his hearing aid, which doesn't work half the time, that I loved his performance. The hippies lob pellets of bread at each other's faces, they're thrilled to be there. I hate this braindead world where people talk about nothing but the price of drugs and Indian chemises. I put up with it because Pierre gets a kick out of it, he gets to try new drugs and spends his days in lotus position beside the pool staring at the sun while I draw beside him. He doesn't want me to touch him anymore, masturbating instead per some Sufi method. He rises with the sun and performs a handstand until noon, eats two grapes and drinks a glass of mineral water, stands on one leg all afternoon, in the evening he watches the sunset upside down, at least I'm sure he won't sleep with any of the girls. He's put on a considerable amount of weight. He wears a turban and a bikini made of the same golden fabric. He looks like a ball, it's baffling that he can stay in a handstand for so long. Ever since he stopped his hormone treatment, both masculine and feminine, his two breasts have begun to sag, he's growing out a thick, limp green mustache (green henna is all the rage); when he sits on his head in the afternoon, his breasts and his mustache hang down in the wrong direction, it's disgusting. He's put on so much weight that I can't fit even a single finger in his belly button anymore. But I love him. He has a split personality, it fascinates me. He'll either sit still for hours, or he'll pounce on me, telling me it's all my fault that he missed out on his youth, tearing up my notebook, spitting on my face, he's leaving me, he's going back to Rome. He cooks me spaghetti with bay leaves, insulting me the whole time, I cry in my wheelchair. He sobs over the stove, adding more bay leaves to the tomato sauce, swearing at me. The onion makes him cry even harder, he throws boiling tomato sauce at my face with the ladle. Why are we renting this clammy house instead of staying in New York, where at least he had a job and fun with Marilyn? It's my leg's fault. If I hadn't gotten into that fight with Marilyn, the snake never would have bitten me, I wouldn't have to spend all day in a wheelchair, and he wouldn't be forced play nurse, we could be in Paris, New York, Rio instead of this shithole, all because my leg was amputated. Coglione! He screams at me. Figlio di una puttana! Pierre, I beg him, crying, Pietro, ti supplico, restiamo ancora insieme! No, no e no! He throws spaghetti in my face, I'm covered in it. Sei contento, adesso, sei contento? he shouts. He smacks me with the ladle, gives me two lumps on the head. Then he calms down just as quickly as he became enraged, he goes and sits in lotus position beside the pool. We receive frequent afternoon visits from Michael Buonarrotti and his wolf, which he leaves outside; ever since my little adventure with the snake, I've become terrified of animals. Michael's in love with Pierre and brings him bouquets of marijuana and hashish candies. Pierre plays the same ignoble game with him that he plays with me, he doesn't let Michael touch him, he pretends to ignore him. The other lives in fear of upsetting him. He sits on the ground across the pool and watches Pierre. Living with a wolf has helped him accept this as his natural position. He lights up his water pipe now and then, passes it to us. He lets us in on all the Ibiza hippie gossip, in the mornings he looks after the hippies' kids, his mission being to teach them nothing and actually prevent them from learning anything, that's how they want their kids to be, not crushed by culture, freer than they themselves ever were. There are already a few exemplary cases, which he sometimes brings around the house, Piggy, Moonie, and Rooney, seven year-old hippie triplets whose Argentine mom has been in the Ibiza prison on drug dealing charges since they were born. Michael takes them to see their mom every day and they kindly bring her tabs of acid. Their dad is a black guy from the States who still lives on the island but went crazy, he doesn't recognize anyone anymore, he's always just playing the same two notes on a trombone in the back of a café downtown, in the wintertime they drape a blanket over his shoulders. They're extremely cute, smiley, have a cappuccino skin tone, dressed in turquoise djellabas. They have adorable little feet, which are always bare, tiny earrings, they go naked into the pool and never stop making a ruckus. Their genitals are small, still hairless. Rooney asks me for cash to get a heart tattoo on his butt cheek. Moonie comes out of the pool soaking wet and clings to me to protect him from the cold. Piggy tickles my ear with a seagull feather until I grab it, playfully nibbling his hand. And so Michael has found another excuse to set himself up at the house, I'm crazy about those kids. And he's crazy about Pierre. Pierre, he looks like a fat foam Buddha, except when he's throwing his tantrums and breaking things over my head, although ever since the kids moved into the house (they sleep all entwined with each other on a mattress next to ours) I leave him alone more often, I no longer make ridiculous scenes because he doesn't want to sleep with me, so he hits me less often. And I'd never dare make love for fear of waking up the kids. I get up ten times a night to put the covers back over them, I kiss their little foreheads, their little necks, and in the morning I wake them up with tickles, they crack up and gulp down their bowls of coffee and milk with croissants making delectable little slurping noises, against

Michael's wishes I teach them to count, they only knew how to count to three. They're fast learners, they're very gifted, Piggy figures out division all on his own using the multiplication table I showed them. I rise up against Michael's pedagogical methods, these kids need to study, then they'll be free to do whatever they want. Michael gives in, he doesn't actually care, all his attention is concentrated on Pierre. Pierre, who doesn't say a word all day, meditates, reads the Bible. Michael starts making ceramics, which he fires in the bread oven which served up till now as his house, he moves into ours, and I have to come to terms with the wolf's presence, she exasperates me. She watches me out of the corner of her eyes and bares her teeth, stalking endlessly around the patio as if in a cage. But the kids love her, play with her, toss her into the pool, and she doesn't bite them. I'm the only one she dislikes, every time she comes near me I smack her on the head with my cane. She barks and bites it but doesn't dare get too close. Her name's Mamma. I realize why this ignoble creature despises me: she raised these kids, who still have the habit of suckling from her. She's jealous of me. I can't kick her out, she's kind of their mom, after all, but I live in fear of the idea that she'll attack me, at last I find a good way of keeping her at a distance: one time I rile her up by clacking her on the head with my cane, she works up the courage to get close to me, and I stick out my prosthetic leg, which she bites, breaking two fangs, and since then she lowers her eyes in my presence, believing that I'm made entirely of metal. Still, I'm cautious around her. Having sold a few of his heinous and poorly-fired ceramic ashtrays to British tourists, Michael makes his foray into sculpture. He sculpts a life-size clay Pierre next to the real one, who has no trouble posing, since he's always sitting still to meditate. This clay Pierre doesn't look like him at all, it's handsome, huge, and as muscular as a Greek statue. I wonder if this Buonarrotti, born in Baltimore to an Irish mother, is even aware of Michelangelo's existence. I hold back from asking him, it might send him into a state of shock. Americans are terrified by family trees, they'd prefer to have been born out of thin air, like my three piglets. One day Pierre announces that he has something extremely important to tell me. To do so, he has us step out of the house, and I have to drag my metal leg all the way over the dunes to the seashore where he sits in lotus position and stares at the horizon. The kids trail behind us with their Mamma, they go off to play naked in the waves, throwing pieces of driftwood for the wolf to fetch, she's thrilled. Pierre declares that he's going to become a guru. He possesses the eternal truth. That's not too worrisome, but I am curious to know what it consists in. Nothing, that's that. But wait, there's another little detail: Marilyn, with whom he's kept up an extensive correspondence all winter behind my back, will be his priestess. That's right, his priestess! She gets in tomorrow by charter. What am I supposed to do? I was so at ease on Ibiza, the kids in good health, Pierre more or less serene, what fresh horror is about to fall on my head? And then there's Michael; how will he react, will he let himself get reeled in by Marilyn, too? Thankfully he's too good a guy, we'll see in what follows that he'll become my ally. She arrives. With purple hair, flowing Greek dresses, all the same color, golden belts shaped like laurel leaves, sandals, she wears floral crowns on her head, all nylon, at night she walks around the patio on acid with a torch in her hand, reciting the *Divine Comedy*. I hope that one day she'll go up in flames with her nylon flowers and her torch. This ridiculous girl goes on mismatching styles and tastes, she hones in on a hybrid of Homer and a little Jewish girl from the Bronx and leans into it with gusto, she wants to make Pierre believe that she alone can furnish him with the special ardor that his new practice requires: he's hypnotized. He takes dozens of hits of acid and spends the whole day staring at the sun, drool dripping from the corner of his mouth. Marilyn, stoned beyond reckoning, kneels before him and reads a bit of Krishna, the kids find the whole thing hilarious from the get-go, dropping pebbles into Pierre's mouth which go entirely unperceived, but I quickly become indignant: this is not a suitable environment in which to raise the kids, even if they've seen it all before at their parents' house, it doesn't matter: Pierre sits still for days, he relieves himself in situ, Marilyn dunks him in the pool to rinse him off with the aid of Michael, who still lacks a well-defined role in this circus: he hates Marilyn as much as I do, but sees that Pierre loves her; either he doesn't dare attack her head-on, or he respects Pierre's absurd decision. I try to get him on my side, we often take the kids out to distant beaches in the 2CV, I learn how to drive with my metal leg, Michael doesn't know how to drive, we let Pierre and Marilyn proceed with their Hare Krishna trip at the house, we bring salads that Michael prepares at home and a thermos with vodka and orange juice for us, another with apple juice for Piggy, Moonie, and Rooney, a water bottle, and leftover pork chops for Mamma. We go off in search of secret coves, I'm not wild about exposing my stump in front of strangers, they're the ones who get embarrassed. We set up our beach umbrella in a quiet corner, I can't handle much direct sunlight because of my stump, Michael can't either since his light, delicate skin burns right away. I start crocheting winter scarves for everyone, it relaxes me, distracts me from my notebooks and my Bic, Michael rolls a few cigarettes with some pretty repugnant weed that he grew on our patio (the tourists buy up all the hash in the summer), he rolls fat, solid spliffs. We chat mostly about the kids' future, we're uncertain about what kind of education to give them, we compare our respective educations, which strike both of us as disastrous, he went to school in Baltimore, I studied in Buenos Aires, but the stories are basically the same, the important thing is to get them away from their stifling family life. With us, they don't have a real family, they've really never had one, they're truly free kids. But at the very least they have to learn to read and write. Piggy, the most gifted of the three, already knows the whole alphabet, Moonie likes building sandcastles, Rooney spends his days whistling the latest Spanish hits he hears on the transistor radio. Piggy will study philosophy (at Vincennes, Berkeley is out of the question), Moonie will be an architect (I reluctantly concede that an American university would be the best option), Rooney will study voice at a Viennese conservatory. The hardest part will be separating them, we tell them of our plans, they're excited but all the same insist that they don't want to be apart from each other. How about when they're older? No, they'll never want to be apart. They'll have to decide on something all three of them like like. A trio of tenors, a trio of architects, a trio of philosophers? (We immediately rule out this ridiculous idea.) We can't think of any example of triplets who have enjoyed success in the same field except for rugbymen, a possibility we fanatically discard, we're tormented by the idea that our three lovely boys be sentenced from birth to our own neurotic burnout lifestyle. The triplets get bored of the conversation and paddle way out on the water to go spearfishing on a little yellow inflatable boat that I bought for them. When we feel like heading home, Michael calls them in with a whistle, we roll one last hash cigarette on the beach, the sun is going down, I hop to the water for one last dip. My stump hurts less, the chill of the waves' foam licks at me, my knee contracts with pleasure, I swim out with big strokes, grab the kids' inflatable boat, which turns over, we're laughing like crazy, getting water up our noses, Piggy dives down and pulls down my trunks, I grab Moonie's legs, Rooney bites my arm, and the wolf swims around us, barking. Back on shore, Michael has already folded up the beach umbrella and put the leftovers in a basket, he hands me a dry red towel, the kids prefer to roll around still wet in the sand, they look like little veal cutlets alla milanese. We stick the deflated boat in the 2CV, I slip on my metal leg, we hop in and set off, howling with laughter. The wolf has finally accepted me into her pack, sometimes she comes over to lick my stump but I won't let her, I'm afraid she'll bite me, I could get an infection.

There's always some scene when we get home: Marilyn doesn't want the kids to make any noise because it disturbs Pierre's meditation, we always end up swearing at each other, I tell them both to just get out and leave us in peace, she slaps me, accuses me of killing her snake, I punch her, she cries. Pierre sits absolutely, and I mean absolutely, motionless in a corner of the patio, he doesn't move at all anymore. He holds his arms up in the shape of a cross, he never lies down, at night we use an extension cord to place an electric heater in front of him, Marilyn sleeps at his feet, wrapped in a leopard skin coat. Piggy has the measles. We separate him from the others, I quarantine alone with him in the loft, I pamper him, meanwhile Michael takes care of Moonie and Rooney and passes us meals through a transom. I don't care if I get the measles, I love this little guy, it's my duty to take care of him and prevent the others from getting sick. He has a fever, he cries, his poor little body is covered in red blotches, he clings to me, I give him a kiss on the lips, calm him down, have him go to the bathroom in a chamber pot. He's delirious, he's seeing little blue butterflies on the ceiling. Piggy, Piggy, I whisper in his ear, be a good boy, be quiet! He falls asleep on my shoulder, sucking my thumb. While he's sleeping, I try to take notes on my novel, but I can't get anywhere with it because I'm so worried about Piggy. I'm not the only one,

67

Mamma keeps me company, we've really become friends now, she brings me the plate of prime rib that Michael passes her through the transom, she doesn't even touch the meat, I give her the leftovers. Now and then, she comes over to lick Piggy's little face, howling, I soothe her, I tell her that he's going to get better, she calms down. The forty days go by, one day Piggy wakes up and leaps out of bed, his red blotches are gone, he throws himself around my neck, laughing, bouncing up and down on the bed, the wolf barks with joy, he's cured. We throw a little party and invite some other hippie kids around the same age, Michael and I make a huge birthday cake and hide Moonie, Piggy, and Rooney inside it, we serve it out on the patio. The three boys jump out of the cake, singing: Silent night, holy night! It's Christmas, there are presents everywhere, little chocolate bunnies hidden in every corner, all the adults are on acid, Pierre attempts to communicate with the beyond and gives a speech in Esperanto. Marilyn and I have made peace, I received a prize for black humor in Paris for an old book of mine, my standing has risen, she's free to invite over the old hippies completely puddled on acid to whom Pierre reads Sufi texts while Marilyn bathes them in incense smoke. The kids go out begging for money with the wolf, they taught her to hold a hat in her teeth. Marilyn's set up a profitable little endeavor. She puts everyone to work: the kids, Pierre, Michael, the wolf, myself. After being chased by the New York mafia, which she owes a shipment of weed (she spent it all on dresses and fur coats for herself), she came to hide out at my house on Ibiza while reestablishing her network. The old trannies from Paris start turning up, they marry old hippies for Spanish papers (anyone who gets married on Spanish soil automatically becomes a citizen), I see the whole old guard of Le Carrousel, Leslie's, and Madame Arthur walk the aisle in my house, wedded in extremely pedestrian Baptist ceremonies (they dip their feet in the pool), the old hippies with twenty years of drug use behind them don't even realize they're trannies. Led by Marilyn, the girls take over their shops, swap their artisan-leather style for something more nylon-bimbo, soon they own three storefronts on the Paseo del Rey Juan Carlos. They stop German tourists in the doorways of their boutiques, dressed like gypsies, they read their palms, invite them into their shops, sell them Michael's ceramics, claiming they're Greek vases they fished up from a ship that wrecked on the Ibizan coast three-thousand years ago. Michael and I can't stand this world, we decide to remove the kids from it, they've become true brutes in the meantime, they go out begging for change on the street with the travestis, we just can't keep track of them anymore. We decide to have a serious conversation with Marilyn, we don't mind if she and Pierre are on a Hare Krishna trip but we don't want the kids shaving their heads and begging for change at the port whenever the tourist ships come in. Marilyn has some Polaroids of me giving the kids kisses on the lips, sleeping all intertwined with them: she blackmails me: I have to marry her or she'll report me to the Spanish authorities, I'll go to jail, the children to a juvenile facility. I beg her just to go away with Pierre, to leave me and Michael with the boys, I'll pay her a monthly pension. But no, she wants to marry me. I committed a tactical error, she's spent years pretending to be in it for Pierre: but it's been about me all along. It would be crass to think she wants me for the money I make on my comics, false to think she loves Pierre or the kids, the simple fact is that she hates me, this is all about her hatred for me. Why does she hate me so much? Not even she knows why, she's simply hated me since the first time she laid eyes on me, her love for Pierre has been nothing but a ruse to fuck with me. She's no longer interested in Pierre, now she wants to torture me by way of the kids. I'm forcibly married to her in the Ibiza Cathedral by a ghastly ninety year-old priest, I've rented a tailcoat suit, she's in white with a veil and orange blossoms in her hair (the fact that she married Pierre five years ago in Amsterdam doesn't appear to bother her at all), the kids and Michael have to wear ties in order to attend the ceremony, the old braindead hippies throw rice at us while we process out the doors, I sob with impotence and rage.

6

The Crystal Ball

I find myself walking alone down Boulevard Magenta, not sure where I'm going. I ring up Marielle de Lesseps from a sidewalk phone booth. What time is it? She has no clue, neither do I. Marilyn's dead, I tell her. It's in *Ici-Paris*. Which Marilyn? she asks. Not the one you married, is it? The very same. Shit! she says. I'm so sorry. Can you find out under what circumstances she died, and what the true story is? Marielle has access to all the telex info. This could turn into a political scandal, a French citizen hanging herself in an Italian jail, I want to know how she died, I'm kind of her widower, after all. Hold on a sec, Marielle says. She calls Rome on another line, it's always busy. Hey, and what if I ask her mom? Her mom? Marielle knows Marilyn's mother? Is she the same Delphine Audieu who used to perform that pathetic little number at the Alcazar? The very same. She's in my novel, Marielle says. But she was my wife, I want to know how she died! I thought you were in love with Pierre, Marielle says. True, but I still need to know how Marilyn died. Her mom's the mother of the lady at the bakery I go to, Marielle says. Where's the bakery? Boulevard Magenta. Near the Gare du Nord? de l'Est? A bit to the left. Right in front of a public phone booth. That's where I'm calling from, as it happens. Well, the bakery is across the street. Madame Audieu? I ask the baker. She shouts Madame Audieu into the intercom by the register. Madame Audieu comes down. Monsieur, she says to me, I saw you from the window, you were in the phone booth. I was sure that I was the one you were looking for. Come right up! This woman's resemblance to Marilyn is striking, she's exactly the same, only without makeup and thirty years older, her hair's white, she's dressed in black and has pink slippers on. She's a psychic! She keeps her crystal ball on a little circular table, a stuffed owl on a perch. Don't be alarmed by the decor, she says, have a cup of tea. What's your line of work? I draw comics. She stares at me while the water heats up. Has she read the morning *Ici–Paris*, does she know that her daughter's dead? Maybe they'd been out of touch for a long time. The woman at the register looks like her, too, she's Marilyn's sister, with an extremely complex blonde hairstyle that must be difficult to maintain. Her name's Corinne. She comes upstairs to tell her mom that her daughter Joséphine (who's fifteen) will be handling the register while she steps out for lunch at the snack bar. Her mom asks her to pick up some batteries for her crystal ball. Are you a Capricorn? she asks me. Virgo, I say. She throws my tarot. She doesn't even notice that I'm gay. There's a woman in your life, she tells me, not an inkling that it's her daughter. My wife hanged herself, I tell her. She stares at me for a moment, unsure if I'm yanking her chain. Well, if she hanged herself, she says, it must have been your fault! I recognize Marilyn entirely in her outburst, an older version, as if she'd lived all her life on Boulevard Magenta. Any kids? she asks. Three, adopted. Also dead. She takes me for either a reporter or a cop. Just as unimaginative as her daughter. There's nothing wrong with our work, you see, she says, defending herself, we comfort people. I agree, I just want to know my future. Immense satisfaction in your professional life. Does she think our jobs are similar (in her eyes, at least), that I also invent stories out of thin air? See that owl? she asks. If you look at it closely, you'll see your hanged wife. Beside the owl on the mantle, I notice a picture of Marilyn with the owl (the same one that's presently stuffed, or maybe another that looks just like it) on her shoulder. She's thin, with a hooked, aquiline nose, she's a dead ringer for her mom. So, I met her post nose job. Is that you? I ask her. Ah, no, that's my little Delphine, she says, a bit perplexed. Isn't that the Marilyn Monroe impersonator from the Alcazar? Did you know her? she whispers. I was her husband. She leans over on the back of her chair, I think she's going to faint, I help her return to her seat. I knew she had died, she says. I read it in my ball, but I refused to believe it. Pass me my salts, they're on the dressing table. I pass her a little snuffbox. She snorts it, making the same clumsy gesture her daughter used to make to hit cocaine. Little Joséphine pops up to tell her grandmother that a customer would like to see her for a love spell. Mme Audieu asks her to sell the customer a mandrake-infused croissant for fifty francs, to be served to the victim at breakfast tomorrow, she doesn't have the time to go downstairs right now. If the croissant isn't effective, there's always the ninety franc apple turnover. The girl says okay, granny, and hurtles down the stairs to get back to work in the bakery. She's ugly, pointy braids, glasses. She looks like Marilyn in the picture on the shelf. The old woman is just as shrewd at selling her husband's pastries as Marilyn was at hawking Michael's ceramics, the former selling affection, the latter ancient Greek relics. The former on Boulevard Magenta, the latter on Ibiza, all of it baked in a bread oven. I wonder what her dad looks like. Politely, I tell the old woman I'd like to meet her husband, he's kind of my father-in-law, after all. Of course, it's just that he's taking a nap right now, he stays up all night baking the bread, they never see him, they have opposite schedules, Monsieur Audieu sleeps all day by the oven in the basement because of his rheumatism, the mother, daughter, and granddaughter all sleep in here at night on a pullout couch fit for three. On the weekends, they go fishing off the banks of the Marne. I didn't realize you were so young, the mother says. Marilyn had described me as a crippled old man in her letters. I may not be an old man but I am indeed crippled, I show her my metal leg. You can't even tell, American engineering. Marilyn often wrote home to her about her life in New York, she wrote every week. She scrawled on Kleenex, crumpling them into little balls and tossing them into the corners of her room at the Chelsea Hotel, whenever she finished a box she'd stuff it with her writings, sometimes including balled-up Kleenex that had no writing on them at all, just traces of makeup and lipstick. She sent all these boxes home to her mom, who decrypted them as she could and then wrote back. She was the one who convinced Marilyn to buy a snake, they offer fantastic protection against the evil eye. She was born under the sign of the Snake, her mother explains. I gave birth to her right here on this couch. She came quickly into the world, there was an eclipse that night. As soon as she'd felt the first contractions, she knew it was a matter of twins, she sent out her husband for the midwife who worked as a concierge on

Avenue Trudeau, she's not in right now, they give him the address of another midwife on Place Blanche. He finds her, she asks for three francs (the francs of back then) up front, the baker doesn't have enough. He borrows some money from the pharmacist on the corner, signs an I-O-U. The two midwives arrive at the same time, Delphine and Corinne have already been born (Delphine is the future Marilyn, Corinne the future cashier, widow of a baker's apprentice, who has a daughter: Joséphine, the teenager currently running the cash register). Before giving birth, Mme Audieu heard the voice of Saint Anne, of whom she's still a devotee: as soon as her two daughters are born, she becomes a psychic, she starts seeing the future in everything. She witnesses the course of her daughters' destiny: Corinne will work the register, Delphine will become an actress. Mme Audieu's favorite is Martine Carol, young Delphine follows her example, by thirteen she's impersonating her, she goes to the conservatory with Brigitte Bardot, spends six years there, sadly she doesn't land any roles, she kicks up a stink with the administration, one of her mother's customers finds her a job working the register at a queen bar, she changes her style.

She lays eyes on us for the first time in 1965 as we walk into Le Pimm's, she hangs up Pierre's and my heavy checkered coats, hands us two tickets, asks if we have anything in our pockets, she's not responsible for any belongings left at coat check. We stuff our cash and passports into the pockets of our blue jeans (handy!), we keep our address books and checkbooks in hand. Marilyn pours us two screwdrivers, we're the only customers at the bar, the Cinderellas never come out before midnight. We watch a fly buzz around, she turns up the music. Can you turn it down? I shout from the far end of the bar. Nope, that's the way it is! she shouts back. And that's how we met Marilyn, a good ten years ago. Back then, she looked a lot more like her twin sister who stayed behind at the bakery register. We immediately hated her, the same way we hated all those women who started slipping into our clubs back then ('65 or '66?), generally the sister or cousin of the bosses' boy toys. Amongst ourselves, we referred to them as fruit flies. Sometimes they'd solicit the old queens to take them out to hear Callas at the Opéra because, back in those days, some of these sugar daddies still didn't dare go out alone in public with their young gigolos. Once these women had established themselves in coat checks or behind the bars, more of them started cropping up: women with epic pasts succinct enough to recount in this wild atmosphere. They were all widows or divorcees, their ex-husbands had all been effeminate, by now remarriage is off the table (they either waited too long or dove in at a serious cost), but they gladly invite the hairstylist queens to their cocktail parties, introduce them to their higher-society friends, bring them along them to openings. And that's how the snooty lady's queens start coming around. Some hard-up young girls venture in after them (they're the ones who first brought hash around), the American style takes hold of Rue Sainte-Anne. They show up with the latest British hits, soon we're forced to dance, luckily I still had my two legs back then. The prettiest gigolos get married to them, all while keeping their old queen sugar daddies, and by 1970 there are as many baptisms as there are orgies on Rue Sainte-Anne, the happy families often spend their vacations on Ibiza, although without getting too crazy, they're Americanized but more in the style of the young couple, they complement their child benefits with four of five thousand francs from the old man, a number of these families also include an old female of the sort who goes out on the town with younger gay men who pay their rent, sometimes it happens that the queens' old widows and the old widow-happy queens get together, there are even marriages of convenience, for example, you might catch some young girl-queen couples with kids and an old woman-queen couple, something like the grandparents, vacationing together on the Loire. It's pretty sweet.

Back when Marilyn was still serving us screwdrivers, we gave her the cold shoulder, we thought she was unbearable. And she hated us too, charged us twice the price for our drinks. It was around the time she became the reigning diva of the Alcazar (in the mornings, she took a "Marilyn" class with a very fine actress who has since passed, Tania Balachova, on the invitation of a mime, a queen who would later also become a great star of travesti Paris) that we started hanging out with her, which is to say that once she switched sides of the bar she actually made an effort to be funny and kind; that was more than enough for us, all we asked was that she not try to put it in our heads that we were living a shared adventure, or encroach upon our space. How I regret not having gotten rid of her back then, it would have been so simple to slip some arsenic into her screwdriver at Le Pimm's, who would have suspected me? She was very courageous in her career, her mother says. I don't contradict her, although I don't ask which career she's referring to, either. She's the one who says it: her career as a wife. O mother mine, why did you make such a misogynist of me? Marilyn's mom thinks she was one of those girls who marry their sugar daddy because they're actually in love with his handsome and virile boy toy. The daddy (I'm referring to myself in this case, she must take me for an antiques dealer, she tells me that the only queens she knows are essentially secondhand dealers around Porte de Clignancourt), I'm nothing but the taster who discovered this rare pearl of a young man who turned out to be the love of her daughter's life (she imagines Rudolf Valentino), I'm nothing but the older husband who facilitates the whole situation: this dangerous psychic has clocked me as a cuckold queen. I get her talking about the kids: she knows we adopted three, she didn't know they were dead: her eyes don't show the slightest glimmer of sympathy. Those children came into the world damned by their race, she says. I feel my chest swelling with rage, just as it did during my conversations with Marilyn back when we were married, my hatred is so physical that I can feel my stump pulsing. That's why they died in an accident, they had to expiate their father's sin for being black, and for dealing drugs, too. Marilyn hid her dealing from her mother, she didn't believe her daughter was capable of it, she's adamantly anti-drugs, if her little Delphine hanged herself in the Regina Coeli Prison it's because she found herself one night by total chance in the company of people doing drugs, she was just their fall guy. Besides, she wrote home saying she didn't really like the kids, they were dirty and badly behaved, I was the one who forced them into her life because I'm an old pervert. Want me to tell you how they died? I ask her. Something about my tone scares her. Or you'd rather divine it in that crystal ball of yours? I already saw them die in my ball. I watched them get torn apart by a shark with their inflatable boat. Yes, but I saw it happen with my own two eyes. I'd really love to tell you about it. She doesn't want me to, she has heart problems. Shut up and listen, I say. She stands up to call her daughter on the intercom, I shove her violently back down into her chair and close the door. You're going to look into that crystal ball of yours and tell me if you see what I see. But Monsieur, she chokes out, I hardly know you. Have mercy on a poor old woman. I turn on the crystal ball. You see your little Delphine hanging there? Monsieur, she tells me, I don't feel well. My salts! I slap her across the face. I take her by her hair, smash her forehead with the crystal ball, she moans and faints in her chair, she has a huge blue lump on her forehead, a stream of blood flowing from her ear. From downstairs, the usual sounds of the register, I look out the window, Boulevard Magenta, same as ever. The old woman is still groaning, I choke her, she dies, sitting in her chair. I fix my hair with my pocket comb, slip into my raincoat. I walk downstairs. Little Joséphine is still at the register, she smiles at me with her big teeth. What'll it be, monsieur? she asks. A two-hundred franc rum log, I tell her. Her smile widens, she takes me for a good customer. Dad, one rum log, please! One what? a man's voice calls up from the basement after a pause. One what, monsieur? the girl asks me. I repeat: one rum log. One rum log, the girl shouts down the stairs. We've got yule logs, not rum logs, the grandfather replies. That doesn't exist. I insist. Mme Audieu told me very specifically to buy a two-hundred franc rum log. You must be mistaken, the old man says, walking up from the basement, enveloped in a cloud of flour. He looks like an older Michael Buonarrotti, his red hair a bit white, his broken nose, it's all there. We don't put rum on anything except our rum babas. Now, if I want rum on my yule log, that's nobody's business but mine. But nobody does that. He wipes his hands on his apron, vigorously shakes my hand. A customer of my missus is a customer of mine, he says. And he laughs, the girl laughs too: Can I have a piece of gum, grandpa? she asks. After you eat lunch, the old man says. I'm waiting for mom, she went to the snack bar, little Joséphine says. When her mom comes back from the snack bar she goes over there on her own for the second serving. She's a clever kid, never makes a mistake behind the register. Now, for two-hundred francs I can sell you a nice big sourdough shaped like a turtle with candied cherries for eyes, same price as the log but it's easier on the stomach, he really recommends it. I tell him two-hundred francs is too much, he throws in some rum. The girl asks again if she can have some gum, she gets permission, the pink gum comes and goes in her smile, a woman comes in, buys half a baguette, asks if Mme Audieu is feeling better. Why, thanks, she sure is, would you like to see her? She wants to have a session concerning her unemployed husband's future, but she won't be able to pay until tomorrow. I say goodbye, pay two-hundred francs for my rum soaked turtle-loaf wrapped carefully in a page of *Le Parisien*. They let the woman in behind the desk, she walks upstairs. The old man shakes my hand. Take care now, he says. I also shake little Joséphine's hand, she curtsies and says merci, monsieur. The woman who had walked up the stairs comes back down screaming in horror. Right then, Corinne comes in from the street screaming the same screams, *Ici-Paris* in hand. Delphine is dead! cries the one, Madame Audieu is dead! cries the other. One hanged, the other strangled. Gawkers start gathering in the bakery, I take the opportunity to nick a pain au chocolat and duck out. It's nice out, it's fall. I walk down Strasbourg and Sébastopol, hand the rum soaked turtle to a bum and eat my pain au chocolate, I make it to Les Halles, turn right on Rue de Rivoli, go sit on a bench in the Jardin des Tuileries facing the basin, I spark up a joint, a queen winks at me, she has a mustache like mine, only hers is red.

Hi, she says to me. Hi, I say back. She's a theater queen, she's done some miming. I'm Jean-Marie. Nice to meet you. She saw me with Marilyn once at a dress rehearsal. How'd she recognize me? My mustache. I know that's not true, she recognized me from my limp and cane. I don't feel like talking,

I pretend to edit the notebook I'm always carrying under my arm. Are you writing? she asks me. No, I'm editing. Can I read it? No. That cools her right off. Bye-bye, she hums. Once she's far away, I notice that she has a limp, too. What a dope, she's out looking for the love of her golden years. Distractedly, I watch the kids playing with little sailboats on the basin, I close my notebook, I think about the death of Piggy, Moonie, and Rooney.

7

The Mediterranean

Michael and I are sitting on the beach, the little boat sets off with the three boys, the wolf isn't allowed onboard because her howls scare off the fish, so she stays with us, howling from the shore instead. Michael and I, as usual, are saying the worst things possible about Marilyn. Since we got married, she's been shoving her way into the kids' education: she reads them Perrault's fairy tales which bore them to tears (they only like comic books) and insists above all on hygiene, which she herself learned in the States, they should always keep perfectly clean and never eat with their hands, she's always around the house imposing order, she doesn't smoke anymore, doesn't drink anymore, she wears contact lenses, blue jeans and American college t-shirts, sneakers, she has a page boy haircut which she dyes a chestnut red, she puts fake freckles on her cheeks with a makeup brush, forces me to buy her a second 2CV, she paints huge orange flowers on it and drives all around the island of Ibiza, delivering milk and blankets to the children of poor hippies, the trannies aren't a part of their lives anymore, Marilyn's only interested in breeders now, she takes Kodaks on the patio with the triplets and me. These days she makes me share a bedroom with her, though I have nothing to worry about: this thirty-five year old girl is still a virgin. The kids have their own bedroom with a triple bunk bed and have no choice but to sleep in yellow wool pajamas with red polka dots to keep from catching cold. Michael and the wolf sleep in the loft. I detest her. Pierre was checked in to the only detox clinic on Ibiza, which is run by nuns who give him Valium instead of LSD, he doesn't even notice, he's on a trip that he can't snap out of, he thinks he's Jesus Christ, so finds it perfectly natural that nuns would come change his clothes when he pisses himself or feed him baby food with a tiny spoon. He has stigmata on his hands and feet, which the nuns disinfect with alcohol and wrap with gauze. They're used to it, in the next room over there's an Italian who's had this very same affliction for the past decade. Pierre's bellybutton has shrunken to no more than a point, he's gotten incredibly thin, you can see his ribs, he demands a crown of thorns be placed on his head and spends all day fingering a plastic rosary Marilyn bought for him. I go visit him from time to time and bring him pitted olives (it's the only adult food he'll eat), otherwise he swallows them and they have to be fished out, so shrunken has his digestive system become. He has black bags under his eyes and cries all the time. I try to comfort him but he hardly recognizes me, one time he thought I was Judas and called in the nuns to have me forcibly removed. The old priest who married Marilyn and me comes to see him now and then to perform exorcisms, his professional opinion is that Pierre is possessed by the devil, in his moments of lucidity Pierre agrees, and so do the nuns, Marilyn has her doubts, Michael and I don't really care, let him be exorcized. The priest puts the two possessed Italians together (the other is a Garibaldian from Sicily, he doesn't want to be exorcized and they have to put him in a straitjacket), the old Catalan shuffles around the room speaking in Latin and waving a censer, the kids are dressed as chorus boys for the occasion and cracking up, Pierre starts convulsing, blood drips from his bellybutton, it's proof of his possession. All of this only adds to the astronomical sums I pay on rent, two cars, etc., I have no choice but to draw from morning to night for the French papers. The priest offers me a gig drawing for his parish's magazine. No, thanks, I'm a leftist! But I do have to start tightening up my belt at the ends of the months. I put up a show of original drawings in a gallery of some of Marilyn's hippie friends, half the drawings get stolen at the opening, the stoned old hippies piss in the sangria, the wolf bites a member of the Guardia Civil, I have to pay for the drinks and cover the fine, I don't sell a single piece. We're poor, we can't keep up our lifestyle anymore. Michael isn't able to sell any of his ceramics, the tourists only want plastic now. Marilyn refuses to dip into her savings, which is a significant chunk of change (five years trafficking drugs!), everything's in saving bonds for the kids when they're older. I find myself with no choice but to open a knitting business, Michael and I knit ponchos all day, sometimes the kids lend us a hand. But anyway, I'm not complaining, it was a pretty nice life.

The night before the tragedy Michael and I had stayed up late knitting by the fire, which the kids fed from time to time, they play three-way chess matches using an extremely complicated system which only they comprehend. The wolf sleeps by the fire. Marilyn reads a Somerset Maugham novel in a wicker chair. I have a cold, the evening's chilly and we can't heat the house anymore because it's gotten too expensive, Michael prepares me some punch, I'm all wrapped up in a poncho, knitting another. As always when I have a cold, my ex-leg hurts, I'm in a nasty mood, I got the bill for Pierre's third trimester at the clinic. We should bring him back home, I say. It's insane to keep forking over astronomical sums to those despicable nuns just to wash him and spoonfeed him gruel. Michael agrees, Marilyn doesn't. The kids are not going to live with him, end of discussion. She hates Pierre's mystical illness, she wants the kids to have healthy minds. She refers to Piggy, Rooney, and Moonie as Jean-Luc, Serge, and Stanislas. I tell her I can't stand her making all the decisions anymore, I want a divorce. She cackles her American cackle. You'd never dare, she says, and goes on reading through her contact lenses. I feel powerless, I go cry in the kitchen where Michael joins me, he heats me up another cup of punch, rolls me a hash cigarette, the wolf comes and rests her head on my metal foot, I calm down. The kids continue their chess match uninterrupted, pretending not to notice our argument, that's what gets me most of all. Thanks to this diabolical woman's cunning and persistence the kids are growing further and further away from me, she's already planning to send them to a boarding school in England, she's almost succeeded in getting them to desire this great goodbye themselves, so they can study a lot and turn into normal people like everyone else. How I detest her! I sleep in the loft despite my cold, tonight I won't be sharing the bedroom.

The next morning it's beautiful out, summer has suddenly arrived, I'm feeling much better cold-wise, Michael, the kids, and I decide to head off for our first beach day of the season. Marilyn stays behind, she even has the nerve to act upset, she'll be staying home to finish her Somerset Maugham. We can't find our parasol, it's on the patio, covered in mold, we have to wash it, we look all over for our old hemp basket that was so handy for the beach, the old tube of sunscreen. The wolf, who can smell an expedition coming, is going wild with joy. Marilyn asks us to leave some hardboiled eggs and beets for her, which cove are we going to? Maybe she'll come join us later, it depends, maybe she'll feel like staying in to read. We have to stop by the clinic to pay for Pierre's trimester. I get into an argument with the mother superior, Pierre's been haranguing passersby from the window. What's he saying to them? That God is dead. All in all, it's embarrassing for the management. They want us to take him back, either that or he'll be sent to prison. I make a scene, using it as an excuse to refuse to pay for the last trimester, I call Michael and the kids, we put a poncho on Pierre, the mother superior doesn't want him to step out the door until we've paid in full. I pay her for a month, I'll send her a check for the rest (she can wait). We gather up Pierre's things: his rosary and a toothbrush. He doesn't seem to know where he is, we stick him in the back seat with the kids and the wolf, convince him to take a sip of a screwdriver, he smiles. We roll up to an empty cove, we get Pierre out, it's been at least a year since he's seen the sun, he starts rolling around in the sand, he and the wolf howl and play together. The kids blow up their inflatable boat, they set out to sea after hugging us and promising to be good boys and not drown. Michael and I plant the parasol in Pierre's shadow, we hand him his rosary, he counts the beads while watching the inflatable boat drift slowly out to sea. The wolf howls, today she's out of control, she really wants to go out on the water with the kids. Michael and I set ourselves up next to Pierre in the shade, I've removed my leg. I love you, Michael tells me. I feel a shiver run down my spine. Why? I ask. Because you're a good person. I don't know how to respond. He strokes my head. Why? I ask. I love you because I love you, he tells me and gives me a long kiss, pressing his teeth against mine, as Americans tend to to do. I thought you were in love with Pierre, I say. I was, but that's all over now. I love only you, baby. Pierre starts to cry, we give him an olive and a sip of a screwdriver. The wolf howls, running along the edge of the waves, she's dying to get out on the water, we tell her no. I never thought this guy could love me, I'm not very turned on by him, not by his physique, anyway, it's his gaze I like, and his soul too, he's truly kind. But I'm married to Marilyn, I tell him. Let's get out of this hell, he says, let's take the three boys and go! He wants to steal away with me and the little guys and the wolf and leave Marilyn and Pierre behind on Ibiza. I agree. But will he still love me? Yes. So will I. Still, I have some misgivings about Pierre, he was the love of my life, after all, Michael's, too, we can't just abandon him in Marilyn's tentacles. We'll bring him along, too. Where? Who knows, let's just get out of Ibiza. Sweet baby, he says, let's go to Paris. He doesn't know the world beyond Baltimore and Ibiza, I've told him in detail about the Musée du Louvre, he wants to see Paris! Paris, where I haven't set foot since I've had only one, it's been a good two years. Paris, which I love as I love the memory of my childhood, without much desire to meddle with it. I try to imagine a life in Paris with our three little savages, plus Michael, plus the wolf, plus Pierre in the state he's in, plus this Americanized Marilyn, it's just not viable. I try to explain to him that there's no ocean in Paris, it's sad. He refuses to believe me, he's always lived by the sea, he can't understand how a city could possibly be so far from water. I draw him a map of the world on the sand (omitting Asia because I don't know how to draw it), I show him where we were all born, himself, Pierre, and I, where we are right now (Ibiza is a speck in the Mediterranean), I demonstrate to him clearly that Paris is a landlocked point, no ocean at all. He's extremely disappointed, he suggests we give the island of Formentera a shot, two miles off Ibiza. I ask him why he came to Ibiza from Baltimore, after all the two cities are pretty different and far away from each other. He was born next to the Atlantic Ocean, ever since he was a kid he dreamed of crossing it. Ibiza is the only place in

Europe he ever heard the New York hippies, the idols of his youth, talk about. Pierre asks me what time it is in Italian. Le tre, I answer. È l'ora dell'apocalisse! he screams. We calm him down, he sobs on my shoulder, Michael gives him gentle kisses on the forehead, quickly we feel an equal tenderness among the three of us, we start tickling each other, passing vodka and orange juice between our mouths, Pierre coughs and spits the screwdriver into Michael's eyes, that gets us howling with laughter. The wolf too is really howling now, it's unbearable. What could she want? She dragged her pork chop over the sand rather than eating it, and now she's tossing it into the water. She's bounding around the shallows but won't go any further, she looks afraid of something, Michael screams, pointing to a small triangle on the water. A black fin. A shark! he wails. Un pescecane! Pietro screams. It's a shark. Little ones venture into the Mediterranean sometimes, they're generally nothing to worry about. Michael whistles to the boys a hundred yards or so out, they don't understand what's happening. But hearing our cries and the wolf's howls, they get nervous and try to start up their little motor, they're out of gas, they paddle with the only paddle they have, floating around in circles. The shark is also circling near the shore, it smelled the pork chop the wolf tossed into the water. It doesn't dare come too far in, I know sharks are almost blind and don't come very close to the shores where it isn't deep enough for them to turn around, especially one like this, which is much bigger than I first thought, we glimpsed its body when it was briefly lifted by the crest of a wave. The kids are fifty yards out. Pierre shrieks like a Sicilian woman at a wake, I slap him. I have an idea that builds on the wolf's: let's throw the pork chop way out on the water, far off the kids' path! I ask Michael to do it, I can't remember where I put my metal leg, I'm handicapped, I hop around on one foot. My metal leg! Let's throw in my metal leg, too, it'll break the shark's teeth and he'll clear right out. Where is it? The kids are about forty yards out, the shark fin is speeding straight toward them. They scream, the last thing we want is for them to panic. Michael throws the pork chop with all his might, the shark whiffs it immediately, changing course, we see its gaping maw burst out of the sea and catch it in mid-air. We all scream, terrified. My leg! We have to throw my leg! Where is my leg? The fin speeds back toward the kids, they're thirty yards out. The shark crashes into their boat, but then swims away, we all sigh with relief. Where's my leg? The boat is moving in faster now on the waves, the shark comes close to it, but not too close. We find my leg covered in sand, and Michael dares plunge into the ocean up to his waist, he tosses it out, the shark is unmoved, the leg doesn't have any smell. The wolf decides to make the ultimate sacrifice, she hurls herself into the water and swims straight toward the shark, which takes her in its mouth, lifts her into the air, rips off one of her legs, the wolf still manages to tear into its flesh before expiring in a smear of blood. The shark circles her, then lunges and devours her. Piggy is petrified, Rooney as well, Moonie is the only one who remains calm and keeps paddling. When, suddenly, a wave flips the boat. Out of instinct, Michael, Pierre, and I all dive into the ocean, the shark has taken Piggy and is dragging him out to sea, we cry to Rooney and Moonie to come back to the beach, but rather than listen to us they swim out even further, following the shark to rescue their brother, while we swim some thirty yards behind them. But the shark, who has already torn Piggy to pieces, rushes Moonie, heaving him up into its mouth, Rooney shrieks. Come back! I cry to him, my mouth filling with water. Rooney, please come back, Michael shouts, panic-stricken. I take hold of the overturned boat and lift my head just far enough out of the water to see Moonie's lifeless body floating on the surface. And now Rooney is swimming straight at the shark. The shark rips off one of his arms, his tiny body soars into the air like a rag doll, then falls back into the sea. The shark streaks toward me. I await my death, motionless, I can't even react anymore, I let go of the inflatable boat and let myself sink. I watch the shark's white belly from underwater as it leaps and digs its teeth into the little yellow plastic craft, which explodes, the shark gets scared, turns out toward the ocean, and vanishes. Michael and I swim out and gather the little bodies. Piggie has no arms, Moonie is missing half his chest, Rooney's face is ripped apart, we find the wolf's head floating in the shallows, and my metal leg, which had been carried to shore by the waves. Michael and I weep in silence, wrapping their remains in ponchos, there's nothing but the sound of the waves. Pierre presses his face into the sand to avoid having to watch the scene. A bell rings three times. Where am I? It's the big clock in the Gare d'Orsay, ringing out three p.m. Children play in the basin at the Tuileries, one of them has fallen in, a woman is scolding him. I walk to Rue de Rivoli and grab a taxi, I go back to my hotel room on Boulevard Magenta, I collapse on my bed, I toss my leg onto the floor, I fall dead asleep.

8

33 Rue des Trois-Portes

A terrified scream wakes me up. The landlady's daughter just dropped the breakfast platter on me, the coffee's burning my face, I leap out of bed. A dead body! she cries, a dead body! She tripped on my metal leg, she thinks there's a corpse under the bed. I have to assure her that it's only a prosthesis. She sits in the armchair and starts sobbing, she's all shaken up. Someone just told her that the woman from the bakery on the corner, who also happened to be her psychic, was brutally murdered last night, she shows me her picture in *Le Parisien*, they knocked her out with her crystal ball and then strangled her, to steal her recipes. It's a picture of a young Mme Audieu, she looks a lot like Marilyn, there's a police sketch of the suspect, luckily aside from the mustache it looks nothing like me. I think it's time for me to switch hotels and give myself a nice, clean shave. I let her know that I'll be checking out before noon, she'll deduct the breakfast she sloshed all over my face. I hop over to the bathroom on my one foot, take a shower. The landlady's daughter knocks on the bathroom door. Monsieur, she says, a telegram for you! A telegram? Who could possibly know that I'm here? She slips the telegram under the door, I hop over to it on one leg, wiping my hands, I open it, my fingers still wet. I know it was you who bumped off the old laydy. I'm under your window. (Laydy? A mistake or some kind of innuendo?) I say thanks, I wait until the girl leaves the room, she lingers for a moment, peering at my prosthesis, when I hear her close the door to the hall, I open the bathroom door, and I hop over to the window wrapped in an off-white hotel towel, smiling kindly up at me from two floors down is the little redhead with a mustache who tried to pick me up in the Tuileries yesterday. What can I do? First, call my editor so he can find me a good lawyer. Let's wait, it's still too soon. The police sketch may not look like me but so many people saw me at the bakery, I could run into any one of them on Boulevard Magenta. It was reckless of me to come back to this hotel. What should I do about the guy down there? Let him wait, he's not leaving, anyway. I shave. It takes a good fifteen minutes, I have to start by cutting my mustache as short as I can with nail clippers, otherwise the razor just slides right over my goddamn whiskers. I've got to get the redhead off my trail, what if I hightailed it over the rooftops? Unthinkable with my artificial leg. He's still on the sidewalk, he won't take his eyes off my window and every time I open the curtain he smiles up at me. Still, I'm going to try to shake him, I go down to the hotel lobby with a close shave and sunglasses, dressed in a satin patchwork jacket I'd been holding onto for six years and which happened to be in my suitcase, my hair slicked back close to the skull. Not even the landlady and her daughter recognize me at first, the daughter's upset with me: but you looked great with a mustache! So, you're leaving us? the landlady asks. I am. Did you get a lot of work done here? I did, the room was nice and quiet. The daughter calls me a taxi. It takes a long time to find one, it's a busy time of day. *Paris-Jour* is lying open on the counter with my police sketch on display, the landlady's glasses set down beside it. The redhead is walking back and forth in front of the door, he peeps inside, did he recognize me? The landlady turns on the radio: it's the twelve o'clock news: heinous crime against psychic. The landlady turns up the volume. Mme Audieu was an exemplary grandmother, murdered at noon right in her Parisian home by someone looking to steal her recipes, it's far-fetched. The whole family saw the murderer, a thin man with a mustache who wore a raincoat and spoke with an Algerian accent. He is suspected to be one of her old customers recently escaped from a psych ward. A live report from the victim's daughter

(Corinne) makes the landlady and her daughter shiver: the murderer stayed alone in the bakery with little Joséphine after he'd already strangled her grandmother, rather than leaving straightaway he spent a good ten minutes chatting with her, what were his intentions? The grandfather baker's providential, though coincidental, arrival saved little Joséphine's life. Cut to another psychic who complains about the dangers of her profession. Corinne neglects to mention to the cops that her sister Delphine also showed up in the papers yesterday for hanging herself in a prison in Rome, not a single journalist has made the connection between the two tragedies, maybe Delphine's real name hasn't even appeared in the telex. Corinne would rather keep her twin sister's shameful suicide a secret so as not to tarnish the sublime beauty of the crime against her mother, she's worried about losing her customers to the Tunisian bakeries across the street. On that end, I'm in the clear: nobody's going to go rifling, at least for now, through Marilyn's past, let's not forget that I was married to her. No one but Marielle de Lesseps could possibly make the connection, I know she'll find it a little funny, but even if she suspected that I was the culprit she wouldn't dream of turning me in. It's an almost perfect crime, the redhead is the only extraneous detail, do I have enough money to bribe his mouth shut? My editor gave me five-thousand francs three days ago, I only have three-thousand left, I don't know what I spent the rest on. Will that be enough? And besides, is the redhead a cop? Doesn't seem like one, but you can never tell. The taxi drives up, the landlady and her daughter shake my hand, I grab my suitcase. The redhead pushes the door open, tears the suitcase out of my hand, limps over to the taxi. To 33 Rue des Trois-Portes, the redheaded Jean-Marie tells the taxi driver. I heave a sigh of relief, I thought he was bringing me straight downtown. It's my place, he says, I live alone, he puts a hand on my prosthesis, he smiles, eyeing me in the rear-view mirror. What does he want? We roll up to Rue des Trois-Portes, by Place Maubert. He grabs the suitcase from the trunk, pays the driver, drags it up the spacious staircase, I follow him. Here we are, he says on the fourth floor, taking a big key out of the pocket of his panther-print raincoat. He pronounces the sound *ss* like the Spanish *z* or the English *th*, this is one ridiculous queen. I enter a large studio apartment with exposed beams, a kitchenette, a telephone, a mattress on the floor with loud, colorful cushions, she has color TV, everything feels too neat, it feels like no one lives here. Care for a Nethcafé? she asks. Doesn't she have anything to drink? How about an anithette? In the kitchenette, a poster of Michelangelo's *David*. Thanks, I'll go for a beer later. I'd rather she first explain what she wants from me. I

could tell you were a thavage, she says, tossing anis-
ette in my face. Whip me! she cries, tearing off her
panther-print shirt, her back is striped with lashes,
she hands me a cat o' nine tails. Now, wait just a
minute, I say. Just what do you know about me?
She knows everything. She's been following me for
three days, she rented a room in the hotel across
the street from mine on Boulevard Magenta and
watched me with binoculars while I wrote at night,
she saw me come out of the hotel yesterday at noon
and walk down Magenta Boulevard in a daze, I
paused every two steps, gazing at the picture of
Marilyn hanged in *Ici-Paris*, he was trailing me
closely, eventually I went into the phone booth, he
noticed it was all just a pretext for me to make
signals to Mme Audieu, who was watching me
from the window above the bakery. Judging from
my state of excitation, he knew that I was going to
kill her. This perverse queen has spent years dreaming of getting murdered, she's been looking for her
killer, and here he is: she's finally found him: c'est
moi. How was she able to identify me before I had
even committed the crime? She works in a shoe
shop on Rue du Four. I stopped and looked at their
window display three days ago and she saw my eyes
from the other side of the glass, she could tell that
I was a killer. Since then, she's been following me.
She takes a syringe out of the fridge, boils it, asks
me if I want to shoot up heroin before I kill her.

And if I say no to all this? She'll turn me into the cops, it's in my best interest to kill her. How should I do it? That's up to me, she has several torture devices, both mechanical and electric. She walks me into another room that I hadn't noticed before, the entrance is hidden behind a Moroccan tapestry, there's a big kitchen table in the middle, a number of torture devices strewn around, each more elaborate than the previous, a cage with hamsters in it. She takes off her pants, shows me her leg: I can see where her limp comes from, her leg is stuck through with crochet needles. She hands me a pocket knife, asks me to stab her calf, I follow her orders, she gasps with pleasure, lies down on the kitchen table, she tells me to tie a tourniquet around her thigh and saw her leg off at the knee. I can't bring myself to do it, I'm shaking. Pop some amphetamines, she tells me. I swallow a fistful. Tell me how you killed the old woman, she begs me. I make something up: I pissed on her, but first I ripped open her jugular with my teeth. I stick the knife into his knee, prying away the kneecap, he howls with pleasure. Cut my belly, he howls, give me a C-section! I go and leave a kitchen knife over an open flame, while it's heating up I grab a hamster and stuff it up his asshole, he contorts, I go find an ax, I chop off his foot, I set to work on his tibia, his screams are getting too loud, I stuff his mouth with a napkin that's already soaked in blood, the knife is red-hot now, I sink it into his bellybutton, making my way downward, really stirring up his intestines, I pop his bladder, his urine mixes in with his blood and excrement, I stick my hand inside, something's moving, it's the hamster, still kicking, I grab it tight in my hand, pull it back out, it struggles, letting out little birdy chirps, the other hamsters start making the same sound from their cage, I bite into its neck until it stops squeaking, it's dead. The redheaded Jean-Marie is still groaning. I split his skull with an ax blow. The phone rings, I let it ring, it stops, it rings again, it stops and starts again. I cross back through the Moroccan tapestry, I go into the bathroom and take a shower, I have some trouble with the water heater, you have to light it first and I can't find the gas lever, the phone stops ringing, I soap myself up good, I'm covered in dry blood. I like this apartment, it's relaxing. The hamsters are the only pain in the ass, I put them in the oven and turn it on, they stop squeaking soon enough, I turn the oven off. I call up Marielle de Lesseps, what time is it? I don't know, but you called me at the same time yesterday. Seems possible. She apologizes for having given me the wrong address yesterday, Marilyn's mom's bakery isn't on Boulevard Magenta, she confused it with one on Place Maubert. I realize she's wrong in thinking she made a mistake, I don't mention it. The woman on Magenta was murdered yesterday morning before I got there, anyway, it's in the papers, she's sorry for making me go out of my way for nothing. What are you up to? Nothing, we could get lunch if you want. But what time is it? We have no idea, we could grab a bite at Lipp, it's always open. Ah, I got some news from Rome, she says. She didn't successfully hang herself. She was saved *in extremis*: they're reopening the case, it's a shitshow with Italy's laws right now, it's going to be a real scandal. Marilyn is still alive! That's right, I'm not a widower. Hello? Are you still there? Marielle asks. Yes, I'm here. If I'm ever subpoenaed in Marilyn's trial, her family will recognize me immediately. We agree to get lunch. How long till I drop by for her? The time of a shower. Write down my new address, she tells me, I just moved, wait a sec, I'm looking for a pencil. 33 Rue des Trois-Portes, fourth floor, to the left. She's right down the hall! See you soon, I say, hanging up. A troubling coincidence. I wonder if I'm dreaming. I push aside the Moroccan curtain, the macabre tableau with the redhead is still there, it's real. This room is right between Marielle's apartment and mine, one of its doors even opens onto the hallway between the two. I cross the hall, Marielle's door is open, I knock. Come in, she shouts, I'm in the shower. That was quick! The apartment is symmetrical to mine, except there's no Moroccan curtain, the other room is in plain sight, it's a greenhouse where Marielle has set up plants around a garden table, in the corner there's a reproduction of the *Venus de Milo*. The phone rings. Can you pick up? It's my editor. He doesn't sound surprised to find me here. You know that the girl from the Alcazar you married is in prison in Rome for dealing, and that she almost killed herself? I'm aware. And that her mother who was a fortune teller on Boulevard Magenta just got killed by an Arab yesterday morning? As for that part, I pretend like it's news to me. Marielle comes in wrapped in a white bathrobe, takes the phone out of my hand. My editor is angry with Marielle, he gave her an advance on a novel that she still hasn't written. She completely forgot, she begs him for forgiveness. She hangs up. He's such a pain in the ass! We concur, our editor is becoming increasingly intolerable, he's always forcing everyone to write. How about we just eat here? She has caviar and frogs in the fridge, I just have to go grab a bottle of Vouvray on Place Maubert while she gets dressed. I grab a copy of the morning *France-Soir* on my way, pictures of both Marilyn and Mme Audieu are on the front page, Mme Audieu is much older than her daughter, they still haven't put two and two together, but that will come in the evening edition. I throw the paper out without reading it, *France-Soir* makes me sick. Marielle is wearing a beige skirt and a champagne blouse, I ask her how she's managed not to change her look for the past ten years. You look like a rocker, she tells me. You've changed your look in the past three days. I'm a little embarrassed, it's true: whenever I start writing, I feel the need to dress differently every day. Generally, it should be the other way around, she quips enigmatically, lighting a Kool-Tipt. And are you getting anywhere with your novel? Shit, my novel! I left my three finished notebooks at the hotel on Boulevard Magenta on the little black table by the window. Which hotel on Boulevard Magenta? The Royal-Magenta. She has their phone number, she knows the landladies, their mom was her grandmother's baker. The mother picks up. Ah, it's you, Monsieur Damonte, she says, we got into some trouble thanks to you. The police thought they recognized me in the sketch of the psychic's killer, I should have left her with my new address, they stopped by looking for me, she assured them that I'm an honest guy but they confiscated my notebooks, anyway. My notebooks in the hands of the police! I try to remember if I wrote anything compromising in there. Everything is compromising, every last thing! I hang up. You look pale, Marielle says. The police confiscated my novel. Now we've heard it all! she says, pouring me a glass of Vouvray. I didn't even know you'd published it, it came out today? It's hard to explain, I go quiet, she takes my silence as an affirmation. Our editor is going to freak out, Marielle says. Another trial on his back! Our editor's back is, indeed, bearing a heavy load: the phone rings, It's him, Marielle says, handing me the phone. His voice is gentle and kind: I heard all about about your little imbroglio, the Minister of the Interior just phoned, they'd like you to go to the nearest station and kindly turn yourself in, I'll find you a good lawyer. Silence. They'll understand that you've been taking too many drugs lately, you weren't in a normal mental state, we just have to find a psychologist to take the stand, he knows a pretty famous one. I can tell that it's already too late. The crime involving the psychic is child's play compared to the one next door and it won't be long before they find that one, too. I'm as good as guillotined, a lawyer is useless. Thanks, I say, and hang up. What does he want? asks Marielle. He wants me to turn myself in, I answer. Is he out of his mind? she cries. So it's time to start jailing authors now, is it? I mean, he's really gone too far! She's indignant. She goes to get me more Vouvray out of the fridge. We have to write a statement for the papers, we can't just let this happen! The phone rings, it's my editor again. I've received a photocopy of your manuscript from the Minister of the Interior, he tell me, but it's incomplete, where are the final chapters? I haven't written them yet. I'll have all the time in the world to write them when I'm in prison, at least I won't be able to lose them there. What are you waiting for to go to the station? I'll go right away. I hang up. Marielle screams. Three cop cars pull up under the window in a concert of screeching brakes. The police station has come to me. Quick, Marielle says, I have the key to the apartment next door, no one lives there! She drags me by the arm, opens the door I so recently exited, pushes me inside, slams the door shut. The cops are already on the second floor. There must be thirty of them. Mademoiselle de Lesseps? inquires one in a raincoat. I watch through the keyhole. Is Monsieur Damonte here? He left three minutes ago. Where to? He had a plane to catch to Rome. To Rome! They run back downstairs in a gaggle, one of them stays behind to keep watch on the hall, Marielle is forbidden from leaving her apartment. Through the window I watch the cops talking into their little gadgets, they hop in their cars and take off at full speed. Orly must already be crawling with them, everyone who looks like me must be delighted. I turn on Jean-Marie's TV. It's the one o'clock news. Since the eleven o'clock *France-Soir*, Marilyn has doubled her mom in popularity, they still haven't figured out that she's her daughter. No, wait, breaking news: the French woman serving a drug trafficking sentence is the daughter of the Boulevard Magenta psychic! On top of that, they've figured out that the French woman was an actress, they run a clip of her commercial with the boa. Are the two cases linked? Yes! Breaking-breaking news:

it appears that the mother's murderer is the husband of the imprisoned French woman. A rather unexpected development, the newscaster doesn't quite know how to take it: he has to improvise and find a way to fit psychics and drug dealers together into the same segment, it's never happened before. But the missing link is easy to locate: me. A rather drug-addled comic artist, they show slides of my drawings, a picture of the café-theater where I used to drag, another picture of me dressed up like a bear at a party, another of me as a kid at the beach, none of them looks like me, on that end I have nothing to be worried about. If that asshole editor of mine hadn't had the brilliant idea of calling up Marielle today to ask for her manuscript, I'd be free right now. But it's my fault, too, how could I have forgotten my notebooks on Boulevard Magenta! The phone rings. Someone knocks. It's the cop who stayed behind in the hallway. They find him yet? he asks. Not yet, I answer. Are you going to pick up the phone? What phone? Hello, Jean-Marie? It's my editor's voice. I answer in a whisper: Jean-Marie's not home right now. I know it's you, he shouts, where's your manuscript? I didn't realize that Jean-Marie was a writer too. I'll stop by with it this afternoon, I mumble, so he won't recognize my voice, and I hang up. It's my editor asking for my manuscript, I tell the cop, and I start rifling around for it. It's in a Breton armoire. Twenty or so cleanly typed pages. Here, I tell the cop, I'll leave you the key to the apartment, that way you can watch the news, I have to run to see my editor. He thanks me politely. Just one thing, there's a man napping in the other room, behind the Moroccan curtain. Wake him up in a half-hour. I took care to replace the documents in Jean-Marie's checkered jacket with my own, I leave my suitcase behind, too, I say see you later to the cop who's busy watching the news from the hallway, and leave. I slip a note under Marielle's door: I'm perfectly fine, but don't tell a soul. I'll call you pretending to be our editor. If you get accused of a crime, confess to it. I walk down the stairs, I'm on Place Maubert. Even if the switcheroo delays the search by a couple hours, they'll find me sooner or later. I haven't had sex in at least two days. I'll stop by the Continental Baths on Place de l'Opéra, I'll be able to relax a little bit, too. I flip through Jean-Marie's manuscript in the taxi: it's a detailed account of my comings and goings these past three days: here, I can see myself at a restaurant two days ago, looking haggard, mid-breakdown, in the harsh neon light, when I thought I'd looked perfectly fine. It's worthless. I write my editor's address on the manuscript, pay the taxi driver to drop it off, and step into the bathhouse.

9

Steam

They give you a sky blue bathrobe, a locker key, a white towel, politely advise you not to leave any valuables in your pockets when you hang your robe by the steam room door. I smoke a hash cigarette in the bathroom, I head into the steam room, bodies slide against each other in the vaporous half-light; everything's slippery, even the floor. Just what I need with my prosthetic leg. Someone's stroking himself behind me: let's go to a cabin, he whispers in my ear, I've got poppers! He takes my hand, we leave the steam room. It's my editor! You! Here? he screams indignantly. You still haven't turned yourself in to the police? Let's find a room and I'll explain, I say. No chance! Go put some clothes on and get over there. I've killed again, I tell him. His curiosity is piqued. We go to a room, a sort of cell with two foam mattresses, there are several rows of them, that's where the fussy queens go to fuck by twos or threes, or even to do things all by themselves. My editor crosses his legs, lights a cigarette, puts on his glasses. It's the first time I've seen him in a bathrobe, I feel awkward too, I don't know if I should stand or sit, I opt for the horizontal position, looking up at the ceiling. Did you kill Marielle de Lesseps? he accuses me. No, the thought would never cross my mind. I killed her neighbor, Jean-Marie, he was one of your authors. Jean-Marie Sèvres, he cries, you killed Jean-Marie Sèvres, my greatest author? I'd never even heard of him. You've never heard of Michelangelo's *Pietà*? Sorry, I thought he sold shoes on Rue du Four. And what's the matter with that? I forgot that my editor's a leftist. I reassure him, telling him that I sent in his last manuscript with a taxi driver, it should be in his office by now, I tell him what it's about, it should work nicely as a preface to my book. This calms him down a bit, he'll get a free preface out of it. And did you already spend all the money I gave you three days ago? I still have two-thousand francs. So I'll be the one who has to pay the lawyers? It's certain that even if my novel is a hit thanks to my execution, it will never pay off the astronomical fees of my trial. I apologize. You'll never get well, he tells me, and starts pacing around like we were in Fresnes Prison. I feel my chest swell with rage as it did yesterday with the psychic. I take off my metal leg and smash his head in. Poor guy didn't see it coming. He thought that even if I was a murderer I was still his author, that I'd never dare. Blood pours down behind his glasses, he says: Me too, Copi? I take the belt off my bathrobe and strangle him. I position his body to make it look like he's sleeping, all you can see is the white hair on the back of his head, his blue robe and his feet, I step out of the room, hanging the "Do not disturb" sign on the door, I go take a shower, I have blood stains and white hairs stuck to the heel of my leg, then I go to the bar next to the kidney-shaped pool where they're playing relaxing music on Radio FIP. I order a gin and tonic. Here you go, the bartender says. We know each other, he's the same guy who used to work at Le Fiacre a decade ago: Jules, sweet as he ever was. Nice here, isn't it? Queens dance in couples in their bathrobes around the pool, there are projectors, parasols, palm tree paper cutouts, a revolving crystal ball, all a hundred and fifty feet underground. And the best part is you can stay for as long as you want. Some guests stay year-round, for three hundred francs a day you can rent a room that comes with breakfast, a massage, vegetables at noon, a bilingual secretary in the afternoon for those in need of one, a sauna, dinner and dancing around the pool that sometimes lasts until the sun comes up (how can you tell when the sun comes up?), some of the guests get dressed now and then to go out to clubs or see their analyst. I decide to rent a room, I ask for the key to the room where I left my editor's body, Jules goes out to the drugstore to get me a nice spiral notebook and a black Bic, I'll give myself a steam cure, I'll sit here all afternoon writing by the pool, I couldn't imagine a better place to hide out and finish my novel. But what should I do with my editor's body? It doesn't smell yet, but in two or three days' time? The rooms are so warm. Nevermind, I'll figure that out when the time comes. I lock the door to my room whenever I'm not there. I spend my first afternoon fucking in the steam room, enjoying the occasional short nap, gin and tonics, banal conversation at the bar with the other queens. In the evening a traveling sales-man with a soft spot for theater buys me dinner, he tells me about the latest bedroom farce in great detail, it's awfully boring but things are so calm here, so tucked away. At night I fall into a deep sleep next to my editor. The next day I wake up early, take a shower, and have breakfast at the bar with Jules. He shows me the morning paper. I shiver, I'd completely forgotten about that whole story.

I wonder how Jules hasn't made the connec-tion between me and my picture in the papers, but quickly figure it out: seeing all his old customers from Le Fiacre half-naked in the same blue robes around the bar, he's gotten us all mixed up. They're beyond suspicion, angels of a kind. I don't run the least risk here, everyone's anonymous. Marielle de Lesseps is accused of the crime at 33 Rue des Trois Portes: I'm the victim. They believe she's gone insane, they believe she was investigating the psychic's murder and that I was the killer. There's a picture of Marielle having a good laugh on the front page of *Le Parisien*, she's eclipsed Marilyn and, by far, Mme Audieu in popularity. Okay, at least I can relax now, I know she's not going to turn me in. On the third page, a brief item: leftist editor missing: my editor. Another kidnapping? That's rich. And if I were to ask for a ransom? No, what good would getting rich do me, I'm screwed anyway. I've already wasted too much time these past two days, I have to dive back into my novel. All the queens are still sleeping at this time of day, or rather the ones who sleep elsewhere haven't arrived yet, I have the whole pool to myself, I swim for a bit then set myself up poolside, my one foot in the water, I dry my hands on my robe and open my notebook. Jules arrives with a drink, I smoke a little weed. This is the good life, but how long can I keep it up? I'm positive that I'm good as guillotined, just thinking about it makes my hair stand on end. When I picture the trial that awaits me I get even more frightened. Oh well, I'll kill myself when things get too hard, I'll find a way, even if it can be hard for big time criminals, since they're under surveillance twenty-four seven. I'll have to hide a switchblade way up my rectum before they arrest me, apparently they only use a finger for the search, they don't seem to grasp that you can go deeper.

Although, wouldn't they have metal detectors, like at the airport? Jules snaps me out of my reverie, showing me the front page of the day's first *France-Soir*: the picture of Marielle de Lesseps takes up the whole thing, she's all smiles, the headline above: Rue des Trois-Ports killer, great, good for her, she must be having a lovely old time, but within a few hours they'll have noticed that the redhead Jean-Marie Sèvres's prints (I should have burned them off with the blowtorch, am I an idiot or what!) don't match mine, the search will pivot back to me. Surprise on page two: his fingerprints do match mine: that he has the same fingerprints as me seems incredible. I'll sooner believe in the supernatural than in chance. Looking back over how I've spent my time these past three days, I'm struck by several coincidences: I imagine I died yesterday at noon. I was already dead by the time I called Marielle from the phone booth, I killed three times while awaiting my final judgment, now I'm in the queens' Inferno two stories under Place de l'Opéra. My back is covered in a cold sweat. The paper slips out of my hands and falls into the pool, I see Marielle's picture smiling up at me while it takes in water, the newspaper sinks. Feeling alright? Jules asks. Don't worry, I'm fine. No, you're not feeling well, you had too much sex yesterday. It's easy to forget that you get weaker when you spend all day fucking in a steam room, plus I hardly ate last night, it's no surprise that you're dizzy. Go take yourself a nice little nap, Jules says, handing me a sleeping pill in a glass of ginger ale, you have to take it easy. I don't dare say much, I do as he says. I put on my leg, my robe, I head for my room at the end of the hall. It's twelve noon, the queens are stirring, I run into a few stepping out of their room for a shower before they all go have breakfast together by the pool. Some of them already give me a neighborly good morning, when I open the door to my room to go back in the one staying in the room across the hall opens hers too, a tall one with a shaved head: morning, Limpy! It's a term of endearment: morning, Baldy! I say back, and she comes to give me a kiss on each cheek. She fucked my ass yesterday, she has a thick cock. Is your friend still sleeping? she asks me, peeking her head through the crack in the door, which I try to keep just barely open, and she looks for a while at my editor's corpse. Ah, he's old, isn't he? He's got white hair! Is he your sugar daddy? I'm flattered, why, yes, he is. You're not coming to breakfast with everyone? No, we got up early today, we're going to take a quick catnap. For a second I'd forgotten that my editor's corpse was in there, I thought I'd offloaded all my crimes onto Marielle. I have to find a way to get it out of there, I shift his position slightly in case the queen from across the way comes around again and sticks her nose in, which does not fail to happen two seconds later.

She knocks, I open up. Do you have any shampoo? she asks. Come in, I say. She's happy to, she wants to see if we're comfortable, if we have a hairdryer, a good brand of lube, some magazines. How about a threesome? I ask her. She hasn't done her business yet. That doesn't matter, you can shit on his face, I tell her, pointing to my editor's corpse. He's into that? the queen asks. Oh, he loves it. She doesn't, she knows it's fashionable these days, she's not against it, but she prefers to do her business alone. Suck on my stump, at least, I say, taking off my leg. That she loves, she imagines it's a giant cock. But aren't we going to wake up your friend? She wants to blow him, too. But first I smash her head in with my leg, she falls back onto my editor's corpse, I squeeze the queen's throat, he moans, he dies. There, at least I'm rid of a cumbersome witness. I take the key from his bathrobe pocket, I cross the hall, I open up his room. There are plants, a dressing table, a divan, canaries in a cage. Nice lighting, it's charming. There are some photos of her on the wall: she was a bodybuilder. I tear them down and throw them in the trash. I go back across the hall, I grab my vodka and weed, I come back to the bodybuild-er's room and set myself up to write my novel on her dressing table, I don't have much time to lose. But my memory of Pierre is still hazy, I can't remember anything about my first notebooks anymore, whether I left him in Rome, Paris, New

York, or Ibiza. If only I hadn't forgotten my notebooks on Boulevard Magenta! Pierre refuses to come out of my Bic, it's not working anymore. Everything I have to say about him strikes me as insipid: I don't love him anymore. Or maybe it's this lavish decor that's blocking my inspiration, I was more at ease on Boulevard Magenta. I can tell I won't be able to get any work done here, but I go to the pool for a drink anyway, where else is there to go? It's lunchtime, a queen jumps into the pool to fish out a lobster another one dropped in by accident, the rest are roaring with laughter. The one who bought me dinner last night motions to me, she's the traveling salesperson for a stocking company, she spends three days a week traveling around small towns, four days here, Saturday night she's going to the theater, she invites me along. It's already Saturday? It's Tuesday, but it's Mardi Gras. Today, the queens at the Continental are allowed to dress up, they go back and forth to the Galeries Lafayette, tonight they'll have a great ball around the pool. They're all ridiculous bourgeoises, their cheeks turn red when you mention sex changes to them. Where'd the old travestis from the Carrefour de Buci go? Where'd Michou go, and La Grande Eugène? Probably to Pigalle or Buci. It's been such a long time since I cruised on the street, thanks to my prosthetic leg I'm relegated to the crummiest bourgeois strongholds. How I'd love to kill them all, but I shouldn't blow my top, four crimes in twenty-four hours is plenty. No, forty-eight hours. Either way, I take a certain criminal satisfaction in it. I decide to have breakfast alone in a corner of the terrace, far from the others. They serve you a lobster without even asking what you want. Jules is in drag (it's the gag du jour) with a lobster on his head. I can tell it's going to be a big party tonight, no one's even thinking about having sex, instead of going to the steam room these ditsy queens stay in to try on dresses in their rooms. I lock myself away in mine (well, the bodybuilder's) in a nasty mood. Who knows how long I'll be stuck here! I spend the afternoon trying to remember Pierre, but not a single word comes out of my Bic. I cross the hall and look in my room: my editor and the bodybuilder haven't moved at all, it still doesn't smell bad, or hardly: the bodybuilder did shit herself at the end there. I spray the place with Chanel Pour Monsieur, I lock it back up. I hear laughter from the bar, I'll go see what's going on. The ball has commenced. The traveling salesman takes me in his arms. Can't you see I have a fake leg? I ask. We can still slow dance by the pool. She's complemented her bathrobe with a wide-brimmed hat and covered her face with glitter. Jules hands me a party hat, they force me to wear it. Around nine p.m. several groups of real trannies start showing up from outside and making a ruckus, a few of them fall into the pool.

They're high, it's not house style, we're all very proper here, hardly even alcoholics. Jules is worried, he doesn't dare kick them out but they've already stolen a number of lobsters, most of them snuck in without paying. I tell my traveling salesman friend that I'm going to get dressed for a walk outside, I can't handle this scene anymore. I go to my locker, my clothes are nowhere to be found. Now I'm worried, I go and tell Jules. Ah, you're the one in #133, he says. We thought that stuff belonged to someone who passed out and died yesterday in the steam room, they slapped my jeans and blouson on him and shipped him off to the morgue. I'm furious, how am I supposed to leave this place? Jules offers to lend me the overalls he wears to work in the boiler room, I go with him, it's down a story, it feels like the engine room of a transatlantic steamer. Do you realize, Jules asks, how dangerous it would be if this exploded? The whole floor with the pool and the rooms would be flooded with boiling water in less than three minutes. But why would it explode? Someone would just have to turn the thermometer up to 212°, a three-year-old could do it. Thankfully no one comes in here except him, he's the only one with a key. I take off my leg. Hey, Jules, I ask, do you have a screwdriver? A screw's loose on my leg. He bends over to check his toolbox, I smash his head in. I feel bad, he's the only one I've killed out of necessity, without passion. He was always so kind to me! Anyway, let's not think about that anymore. I put the coat on, it actually looks kind of fashionable on me, I borrow Jules's shoes and Renoma leather coat, it's pretty cute. I turn the thermostat up to 212°, I go up the stairs as fast as I can (ah, this damn prosthesis!), I've hardly made it out of the boiler room when I hear an explosion, the door to the steam room has already shattered by the time I reach the hall with the rooms on it, steam piles out so thick that you can't see a thing, everyone's screaming, there are already casualties and serious burn victims. I go as fast as I can toward the pool, the boiling water starts overflowing. I reach the stairs just as the water touches my slipper. Several barefooted queens start shrieking. Some of them push ahead of me up the stairway, still in their long-brimmed hats, but only a dozen or so, the others still haven't realized the trouble they're in. I manage to climb the stairs two by two, the boiling water nipping at my heels, I watch a queen swimming through it, he's screaming and grasping at the railing, I take her hand and pull her toward me, she's so hot that I almost get burned but it's no use, I pull her toward me and see that she's already dead. I let her go, her body falling back into the great kettle. I leave, I'm out on the street. And it's Paris in the month of May.

10

Amnesia

Firefighters show up, survivors in sky blue bathrobes and wide-brimmed hats cry over their lost
belongings on the sidewalk, I take the opportunity
to get a change of scenery, I split. Where to go?
Paris is overrun with queens, I've had it up to here
with them. I go to a phone booth on Boulevard des
Capucines and call Marielle. Where have you been?
she asks. She hasn't heard from me since we had
lunch four days ago at Lipp. So, I must have been
dreaming, after all. These past four days only ever
existed in my imagination! What have I been up to
in the meantime? I have no idea. Let's get together
for breakfast. What time is it? We don't know. I'll
drop by to pick her up. Where does she live? 33
Rue des Trois-Portes. That part, at least, I didn't
dream. On the third floor? Yes, her apartment has
three doors, I can knock on whichever one. I'll give
her time to take a shower, she's only just woken
up. I hang up, I admit, feeling relieved: I may not
remember what I've been up to these past four days,

but the important thing is that I know I didn't kill anyone. My novel may be gone, oh well, but I'm innocent, that's what really matters. To make sure of it I retrace my steps, I watch the front door of the Continental Opéra, nothing unusual, the queens shoot quick glances left and right before slipping in, they fear that some family member might happen to be in the vicinity (their mother, sister, or wife often visit the area around the Opéra, to go shopping at either Le Printemps or Place Vendôme, so they run the risk of being seen entering or exiting the baths). I take a cab. It pulls up to 33 Rue des Trois-Portes, I don't recognize the front door, that's reassuring, but I'm really not appreciating this mixture of dream and reality, I'm afraid I'll be driven to kill, as I was in my dreams of late. But the stairway is the same. And the landing is, too. *Maledizione.* For a moment I feel like running away. I know that even if I'm not a criminal, the way I've spent my time these past four days has been completely erased from my mind, is it possible that I did kill someone? Is Marielle putting herself at risk by spending time alone with me? No, look, I'm the most peaceful person in the world. Those who are violent in their dreams would never hurt a fly in waking life. I'm considering which door to knock on when the one in the middle suddenly swings open, Marielle kisses me on both cheeks, invites me in. The apartment isn't like the one in my dream at all: Marielle lives amidst rubble from the apartment above: the ceiling beams gave way. She's set up a typewriter on a stool in the corner, she sits facing it on a cushion, this arrangement isn't any good for her, nothing comes to mind to write, her novel is still at point zero. She spends her days with her mouth wide open, staring at the gaping hole in her ceiling. It's unlivable, she says. She has an architect friend who wants to turn the place into a duplex, but they can't get a hold of the owner of the apartment upstairs, he's always traveling. Let's go have lunch at Balzar, it's open in the afternoon. Ah, but it's so nice here, don't you have anything in the fridge? Just some Vouvray. Plus two slices of smoked salmon and half a lemon. We share it all, but there's a cat. He dislikes me from the start, he doesn't like Marielle either, nobody knows where he came from, he leaps at our pieces of salmon, he claws us, I hold him at bay with my cane, Marielle opens the door, we shoo him out into the hall. He's an enormous black cat with white whiskers. He must have snuck in behind you, Marielle says. He reappears in the hole in the ceiling, we toss bits of rubble at him, he runs away. He knows a way into the apartment upstairs, he must be the owner's. Maybe he's hungry. We throw him a little piece of salmon, he devours it, he lingers, watching us through the hole above while we eat our fish. The Vouvray is ice cold, it's great. And are you getting anywhere with your novel? she asks. I haven't written a word, but I think about it all the time. About Pierre? I've kind of changed the angle. Want to sit on the rubble? We watch the sunset through the window, the cat comes back, purring and brushing up against one of us, then the other. I tell her as best I can about the dream I had of these past three days. Marielle is surprised and flattered by the role she played in it, the troubling part is that I've become an amnesiac. Since when? Ever since I dropped her off at the paper a few days ago. Was that three or four days ago? Either way, I had a suitcase with me that day, now I have nothing, I don't recognize my clothes, I must have bought them at some point. Do I have my papers? I do, my passport. I still have a little more than a thousand francs from the five my editor gave me a few days ago. What happened to the rest? I'm dressed impeccably from head to toe, I must have blown it all at Yves Saint Laurent. But where are you living? Marielle insists. She's getting on my nerves. If only I knew! For the time being I'll stay here with you, I tell her. I'll set myself up on another stool with my notebook and my Bic, we'll write all day and in the evening we'll go have dinner at Le Balzar. I have to write something in the next three days, I only have a thousand three hundred francs left, my editor won't give me another advance unless I deliver new material. That guy really chaps my ass!

I did well to kill him in my dreams. The phone rings: it's him. He has good news: the landladies from Boulevard Magenta called him this morning, I forgot my suitcase and notebooks, his phone number was written one of the covers. I was so spaced out when I left this morning that they were worried I'd get hit by a car. No, just a little amnesia attack. But does that mean that I was writing these past four days? That's right, he just received my three notebooks, full and without a single word crossed out. He read them, he's a little miffed by the role he plays in them. And it's pretty damn snobby, he says. He's not sure he wants to publish it. He'd have liked something more confessional: after all, it's a novel about queens. I promise him that I'll add one last chapter about love. Exactly, that's what the reader's missing, I open with the promise of a love story and fall, as usual, into my personal obsessions! Writing's not worth the trouble, Marielle has a tape recorder. But we're hungry now, let's go for a bite at Ping-Pong, it's a Chinese place in the neighborhood that stays open late. The Asian waiters dress up like tennis players, they serve your food on rackets. We share an order of sweet pork and banana fritters, we drink hot rice wine.

11

With Heart in Hand

I didn't realize you were so rich, Marielle tells me. Was it a real diamond? It was real, and it was huge. On Ibiza, Michael and I found a diamond on the beach. We sold it to Cartier for less than it was worth, they got twenty-three eighteen carat stones out of it, but it got us back on our feet, we left Ibiza for Rome, we're thinking only of Pierre's recovery. Marilyn stayed behind on Ibiza, we're through. A comely waiter approaches to torch our banana skewer, we fall silent. When he leaves, we pick up the story again: leaving Ibiza was more or less painless. Three years of hippie life is too long, all things considered. Rome? You'd think we'd never left, Pierre's just a bit older now, that's all. We rent an apartment with three big rooms on Piazza Santa Maria in Trastevere, it's right by where Pierre was born. Michael adopts the bourgeois Roman style, he picks up some beige gabardine summer suits, some camel fur winter coats. We buy holy water nonstop, in the middle of the biggest room we set up a Pompeian tub where we bathe Pierre throughout the day, he's started talking again ever since. He says "biberon," "piazza," "soffitto." On Sundays we bring him to Vatican Square to see the Pope on his balcony, he loves it, he kneels and prays. Michael takes classes at a sculpture school, spends his days in museums. As for me, I've stopped drawing comics, I'm tired of them, I just clean the house all day. At night we go out for ravioli on Piazza Navonna, I've put on some weight. Michael has become friends with another American named Steve Morton, he's cute, really small and muscular. Unfortunately, someone stabs him to death in a heinous crime, for a good week we're terrified we'll get raided by the police, we hide the hash under Pierre's bathtub. One day Michael comes home all excited: he has a great idea for how to get his name printed all over the Roman papers: he's going to dye the fountain red on Piazza Santa Maria in Trastevere (all it will take is some food dye), we'll dress Pierre up like Christ and dip him in it, it'll make for a nice little scandal. Pierre refuses, he's afraid of catching a cold. Michael is furious, he accuses us of not being in solidarity (*essere solidale*) with his projects. I'm fed up with Michael, ever since he arrived in Rome he seems to think he owns the place, he's back on his artist trip: whatever horseshit they come up with, they expect the automatic admiration and participation of everyone around them. Let him go dye his fountain on his own, we don't like scandals, anyway! Michael slams the door on his way out, goes for a drink on Piazza del Popolo. Pierre has completely forgotten that he was once named Pierre, a travesti in Paris, saggy breasts, at his age, are common among Romans. He's already relearned to read, write, and count on his fingers, he speaks only Italian. I tried to get him to reconnect with his childhood friends: he has none. Romans have only their acquaintances and their families. Pietro has no family aside from Michael and me. Both grandparents on his mother's side died together a decade ago after forgetting to turn off the gas. They're buried in the little tomb in Marinella with Pietro's supposed mother and father and my dearly departed leg. On Sundays, Pietro and I visit them and swap out the flowers in the vases, Pietro prays, I pretend to do the same so he won't get upset. Still, I'd take his religious trip over Michael's artist trip any day. Pietro and I are just two regular guys, blue jeans and sky blue cotton t-shirts, loafers, navy blue shetland wool sweaters which we sometimes tie over our shoulders, but Michael: what a sight! Beige gabardine bell-bottom suits that accentuate his ass, the jacket tight at the waist, epaulets, a long slit in the back, high-heeled boots, frilly lilac satin shirts, he blows out his hair which has grown down to his shoulders, and has an atrocious red mustache which he never stops combing. He's joined a movement called "arte e liberazione," which is made up of some overgrown Italian art school types who dye Venice's water green or the Donatello's *Puttino* red, they go to jail, calls for their release rain down, they're released, they've gotten enough publicity to be able to sell retouched photos of buses in galleries. Michael has two mistresses, one French, the other Italian, Laure and Patrizia, who move into the house only to bicker to no end. This supremely gay man has fallen into the women's trap. That's what the artist scene is like, and especially in Rome. Laura's a hippie, she works at a shop run by a Brazilian where they sell the Chinese clothes he buys in Morocco, Patrizia's a feminist, she lives at her mom's house and works for the leftist papers, she always going on about abortion and the phallus, they resent each other and hate everyone else, what are they even doing at our house? They're fucking Michael, that's what. What do they see in him? Whatever the case, they can't possibly be attracted to such a tiny cock, and anyway, Michael is a terrible lay, he gets it up once a week and cums straight away. They like him because he's an artist. Ah, these Roman women! Although, in a way, I'm actually really happy about it, I get Pietro all to myself. We sleep entwined, giving each other little kisses whenever we wake up or change positions, I lick his neck, he caresses my ass, I suck one of his breasts, we fall back asleep. A few years go by like this. You were actually in love with that moron? Marielle asks me. I was, madly, like a madwoman. Why? she asks. I really don't know. My last guy was an asshole, too, Marielle says. And I couldn't help falling in love, either. I guess it's just what happens to daddy's boys. To mama's girls, Marielle corrects me. We share a ginger crepe and a bottle of champagne, we've had enough sake. We talk about other things, we go home with Peking duck leftovers for the cat. I lie down on a mattress on the floor in the middle of the rubble, Marielle on another with the cat, which never wants to be apart from her again. Thankfully, Marielle's ex left some clothes behind, including some nice blue silk pajamas and a floor-length white bathrobe. We roll a couple fat joints and we chat.

Pietro has recovered enough from his drug use to get a job (it wasn't his choice, of course, we threatened to kick him out otherwise) in a little theater subsidized by the Vatican on Borgo Santo Spirito where they stage the lives of the saints. They cast him because of his resemblance to Christ, he acts only on Sunday afternoons. All he does is walk around the stage carrying a cardboard cutout cross on his back while extras pretend to flagellate him. In the second act he hangs stock-still for an hour on the cross while the Virgin and Mary Magdalene argue over who should get his corpse, in the third act he lies on the ground until an extra lashes a rope under his armpits, they lift him into the air, the nuns in the audience burst into applause, he comes out to take a bow in a bathrobe, Michael thinks it's ridiculous but I find it charming, and anyway, Pietro's happy. By dint of love and a patient touch, I've managed to fit my tongue back into his belly-button, which had contracted so much, I can already get the head of my cock inside, it still hurts him a little, he's not used to pleasure anymore, it's the last thing to come back for acid heads. A year of effort to be able to fit my hand inside, then my stump, which hurts me at first, but in the end we share nearly constant spasms, we give it all we've got.

We don't go out much, Pietro has taken back up his habit of dressing like a woman around the house, it's all very modest, little sky-blue dresses, aprons, slippers to keep the parquet flooring spick-and-span, he spends his days cleaning and leafing through Roman women's magazines, there are enough for the whole week. As for me, I start in on my second novel project. Nothing but images from Italian TV come to mind, I can't get anywhere with it. Michael is frustrated too, he doesn't have any ideas, either they're ideas someone else has just come up with or someone steals his ideas just before he's able to do anything with them. He was thinking of wrapping the fountain in Piazza Navona in green plastic, he made the mistake of talking about it at a hip café, the next day the very same fountain was wrapped in red plastic and signed by another artist. There's a spy in the house. It must be one of the girls: Laure or Patrizia, one of them is selling off Michael's ideas to his rival (Lucio da Vinci, a man from Milan who came to art by way of photography). We decide to investigate, the traitor is Laure, she's sleeping with Lucio da Vinci, who promised to paint her portrait. She gets run out of the apartment suitcases in hand, Patrizia the Italian now reigns supreme. My God, a new, feminist Marilyn! And she's anti-queen, to boot, she accuses Pierre of copying her, Pierre cries, I smack her, Michael kicks me. I tell Michael and Patrizia to leave with their share of diamonds. Good riddance. Pietro and I are alone now, finally, the thing I've been dreaming of my whole life has come true: Pietro has become a woman again, only a bit heavier now, less graceful, easily mistakable for a forty year-old Italian woman from the South, his smell has generally mellowed, his frizzy hair, which he wears in a bun over the back of his neck, smells like bay leaf, his armpits like garlic, his feet like mozzarella, his belly button a bit like fried fish. He puts on his makeup, puckering his lips, soon he abandons the magazines for the lives of the saints, he leaves the apartment only on Sundays to go to mass and then get dressed up for his role as Christ in the nuns' little theater. One of them, a Carmelite, takes a liking to us, Suora Angelica dell'Immacolato Sacramento, the daughter of Milanese industrialist, repentant dyke. She comes by every evening to pray with us before going back to her convent, she steals hosts for Pietro. Pietro wants a definitive sex change, he's decided to become a Carmelite nun. I'm beside myself, I'd love for him to have a sex change, but then for him to become my wife. Instead, he wants to become a Carmelite to expiate my sins. But I haven't sinned! Of course I've sinned, terrible sins, isn't Pietro himself one of them? I found him, a virgin boy, and look at him now, ten years later, an assfucked travesti, is that not a sin? Suora Angelica agrees, she knows a clandestine surgeon who performs cock removals, how awful, I beg them to abandon the project, Pietro's mind is made up. But how could it be possible for the Carmelites to welcome a crossdresser into their order? He wouldn't be the first, per canonical law Pierre's operation will return him to a state of virginity. It's a pretty common thing in Sicily. The mother superior visits us to comfort me, she stays for tea, assures me that Pietro will be happier with God than he is with me, his conscience will finally be at peace, citing the case of Suora Angelica, who, after a troubled youth, found peace at last in the convent. She and Pietro will live in the same cell, I'll be able to go however often I'd like to watch them praying on their pallets through a tiny window. Pietro will go to Hell otherwise, and so will I. Personally, I'm not worried, but Pietro is terrified. He's not afraid for himself, he's afraid that I'll be damned for his actions. But we love each other, everything we've ever done together has been done out of love! The date of the operation is set, I concoct a plan to chloroform Pietro and sneak him out of the house the night before, I'll hide him at Michael's, I've kept him in the loop, plus he lives in the building next door. Suora Angelica, in the final week, becomes increasingly hysterical, she convulses all day, we put her under a cold shower, she shivers in her sopping habit, the mother superior performs an exorcism, the devil is in our home. We have to rid Pietro's body of the devil as soon as possible, his cock is the devil. The clandestine doctor (*il dottore* Peppo) receives some ten thousand dollars in diamonds for the job (it's almost everything we have left, five thousand or so will line the Carmelites' coffers). Pietro's operation will take place at home next Tuesday, they'll cut off his genitals and enlarge his prostate so that he'll be able to pee through a tube which he'll keep in for a few months, then, once his prostate has healed, they'll remove the tube and Pietro will enter the Carmelite order under the name of Sister Madalena del Cuore di Gesù. I ring up one Milanese lawyer after another, no one believes me, I'm basically a prisoner of the Swiss guards in my own home, the Carmelite mother superior presides over my living room, advises Doctor Peppo on the kind of anesthesia that should be administered to Pietro during the operation, she'd rather he operate without anesthesia, it's a kind of birth, he must suffer. Doctor Peppo, being an atheist, compromises for the use of local anesthesia, the mother superior and Suora Angelica will hold his hand and pray for him throughout the operation. Suora Angelica is experiencing increasingly frequent convulsions, they have to smear her with nightshade and flagellate her, she sleeps on a blanket on the kitchen floor where two barefooted religious nurses belonging to a silent order have already begun setting up a rudimentary operating table. This is the last Saturday I'll ever spend with Pietro, I ask the mother superior to grant me one last night with him, she refuses, I threaten her with a scandal, she knows that's impossible but something moves this perverse woman's heart, she compromises, perhaps because she knows that I'll suffer all the more for it in the long run. Two Swiss guards will be posted at the door through the night to prevent us from fleeing. I walk into the room carrying a tray with two slices of prosciutto, sparkling red wine, a cream cake. Pietro is on the bed in a white lace nightgown, his hands clasped, his eyes glazed over. I tiptoe over to the bedside table and set down our last supper. Sei tu, amore? Pietro asks. Sono io! I sit on the edge of

the bed, I take his hand in mine. Che ore sono?
È notte, I tell him. Voglio vedere per la finestra,
he says. He leans on me, we make our way to the
window, open the lilac moiré curtains, all of Rome
is there on this summer night, the smells and shout-
ing, the fountains, Capitoline Hill, the Vatican, the
stairs of Piazza del Popolo, a mandolin, Allora la
vita è così? he asks me (or himself, I'm not sure how
to respond). È tutto questo che si dee abbandonare,
tutto questo! He rests his head on my shoulder and
cries. But no, I tell him, let's leave together, weren't
we happy in Paris? Parigi! He can hardly remember, he confuses it for a suburb of Rome. L'unica
felicità è quella dell'eternità! I hear voices in the
living room, I go to see what's happening, Suora
Angelica has fallen into a trance, she's contorting
all around the room, the two nuns restrain her,
give her an injection. I take advantage of the fact
that the mother superior and doctor Peppo have
stepped out for midnight mass to bribe the Swiss
guards, they'll let us make love without telling the
mother superior. I ask Pietro to put on his pale blue
negligee, he lies down on the red velvet couch under
the window, he picks up his glass of spumante, I
kneel at his feet. È troppo tarde, he murmurs to
me, non sono mai stata me stessa (I've never been
myself, in the feminine), bisogna concludere (this
needs to end), io so che tu mi ami (I know that you
love me) ma io non sono io (but I am not myself),

dimenticami o amami in lontananza (forget me
or love me from a distance), io quasi non esisto (I
barely exist), è per me arrivato il tempo dell'assenza
(absence). L'amore? L'amore! He throws his wine in
my face, che amore? He stands up on his own, leaning on the window sill. Cos'è l'amore. L'amore è nel
passato! I crawl to his feet, sobbing. Ma il ricordo!
We still have our memories. Which? What memories? Niente! Niente insieme. We've lived nothing
together. What about Ibiza, New York, Parigi? È
stato un sogno. (That was a dream.) I help him sit
back down on the bed, his heart pounding. Non
sono io, devo essere forte per più tarde (I'm not
myself, I have to stay strong for later). Ma il mio
sogno d'amore, non ho diritto neanche a questo?
(Do I not have the right to dream of love?) No. I've
already dreamt it, il mio sogno d'amore, it's over.
He lies back down, brings his hands together, he
prays. I slip in beside him under the covers, I cry on
his shoulder, I know it's our last night together. He
falls asleep, snoring. I slide my lips over his body,
take his tiny cock between my dry lips, he gently
pushes my head away with his hand, turning over.
I take the opportunity to press my face into his ass
and tongue his asshole. No, he murmurs, per favore.
I get hard, nibbling on his asscheek. He's asleep,
or at least faking it, again I suck his cock and his
soft balls, then his pubic hair, then his bellybutton,
sticking my tongue inside. Sei pazzo, cosa fai? I slip

my fingers in, he contorts with pleasure, I suck on one of his breasts and stroke his cock with my other hand. Ma cosa fai, ma cosa fai? he murmurs. I push my entire hand into his bellybutton. His intestines contract, his breath staggers, he takes my arm and thrusts it into his bellybutton up to the elbow, it's the first time I've been so deep, my fingers gently part his lungs, I reach the heart, stroking it with my fingerprints, encircling it with my fingers, Pietro murmurs amore, amore, we fall asleep.

Bells wake me in the morning, as always in Rome, but today they keep ringing, it's Resurrection Day, it seems. My arm is cold, Pierre is dead. I try to pull my arm out from the inside of his body, which has contracted so tightly that I imagine that my arm has been swallowed by a reptile, I pull, I manage to get it out, I scream in horror, a Swiss guard opens the door: è morto! We're panic-stricken, the entire house comes into the room, Suora Angelica wraps herself around Pietro's body and falls into a fit of convulsions. Pietro's body, which has become as hard and rigid as a statue, not a single drop of blood flowed from his bellybutton. A miracle! cries the Swiss guard, crying on his knees. Un miracolo! Everyone is weeping, everyone is wailing, even the sisters sworn to silence. We wrap Pierre in a sheet, we carry him out to the street, we go to dip his corpse in the Fontana di Santa Maria in Trastevere, we pray aloud, people gather round.

We bury him the next day in the little tomb in la Marinella which I decorate with chrysanthemums year-round. Michael stayed behind in Rome. He married Marilyn, his tiny cock finally got the better of her virginity, they have a daughter named Pierina, I'm the godfather. I see them sometimes when I come to town. Marielle is asleep on her mattress, the cat purring at her feet. The tape player is still spinning, I unplug it. I get dressed on tiptoes, put a cover over Marielle, turn out the light, step out to the street. The sun is rising, I cross the Pont Marie. Notre-Dame is just opening, tons of old folks are rushing in to enjoy it in peace before the first tourists arrive, which doesn't take long: Japanese people come piling out of a bus. What am I doing here? I buy some popcorn, the pigeons chase me, I cross the parvis of Notre-Dame, I go for a stroll in the Square du Vert-Galant. I shudder, watching the dead body of a cat float past in circles. I cross the Pont Neuf, make my way up Rue Guénégaud, step into a little hotel I know at the Carrefour de Buci, it's the place where Marilyn was living when I met her. The landlady finds me suspicious even though she recognizes me (or maybe that's precisely why) and has me sign a lease and pay up front, I don't have any bags. I walk into a room I don't so much as look at, I sink into the bed and fall asleep without even taking off my leg or my coat.

12

The Last Pissoir

I wake up, I should have taken off my raincoat before falling asleep, I'm drenched in sweat. A red neon flashes on and off beside the window, my head kills. I have no idea where I am. I sit up on the edge of the bed, I try to get my memory working but it's no use. I look out the window, I recognize Rue de l'Ancienne-Comédie. What time is it? Between midnight and three a.m., judging by the street activity. There's a sink, I stick my head as far as I can under the open faucet. I find a towel, I unbutton my shirt and sponge down my chest, I lie back down. My stump hurts, as it does whenever I fall asleep without taking off my prosthesis. I close my eyes and take a deep breath, I'm nauseous. I puke next to the bed, I don't have the strength to get up and make it to the bathroom. What have I been doing these past few days? I wrote, I killed someone. Whom? I have no clue, but I'm sure that I killed someone. Oh well, it will come back to me. I feel better after throwing up, but the smell is unbearable, I wash my face, run some more water through my hair, I step out of my room, I walk downstairs, I leave my key at the desk, I go out to the street. In my pocket, a thousand francs and my checkbook. Where should I go? I head into a café, get a token at the counter, I call up my editor at his house, he was about to go to bed. Your novel is terrific, he says. It's really moving, although he would have liked a less abrupt ending. What novel? The one Marielle de Lesseps gave him today, four notebooks and two tapes. I don't remember recording them. And yet it's my voice, he holds the tape player up to the phone, that's my voice, alright. You can swing by for another advance tomorrow. I say thanks. I go to the Drugstore Saint-Germain, which is still open (it's one a.m.), I buy some underwear, a t-shirt, some socks, toiletries, a tube of Alka-Seltzer, a tube of Hyalomiel, shampoo, I go rent a room at Hôtel Crystal on Rue Saint-Benoît, that should bring back the adventures of my youth. The overnight receptionist recognizes me, I ask him how he's been. His legs are giving him trouble. I one up him, they cut mine right off! I flash him my metal leg, he's almost jealous of it, at least that can't hurt like a real one. I reassure him, it hurts pretty bad, after all. I've slept in this room before, but when and with whom, I don't recall. I take a shower. It's true, my stump has been hurting more since Pierre died. I'd worked up a sensitivity in it with him, something like that of a circumcised glans, ever since he died it's not sensitive to pleasure anymore, only to pain, it gets inflamed if I walk too much for two or three days in a row, the prosthesis bothers it. Oh, it doesn't matter, I'm in a good mood, I whistle a tango in the shower. The fact that I finished my novel eases my mind, it feels like I woke up from a nightmare. I wonder what I'll think of it when I have to correct the proofs, will the reader be able to tell that I forget everything I write? Whatever, good riddance, another novel, another advance. My editor will sleep easy for at least a week until he asks me for another. Maybe he won't dare anymore, for fear that I'll kill him for real next time. The phone rings. Who could possibly know that I'm here? It's Marilyn. She and Michael are staying at Hôtel Crystal for a few days, they're just in from Rome. They were looking for me all over Paris and the concierge told them I'd just checked in. They're staying down the hall. I tell them to wait for me to get dressed. What a setback! Here I was, getting ready to spend my night alone in Paris in the American college tee I just bought down at Drugstore Saint-Germain! I open up, Marilyn waltzes in carrying little Pierina, who gives me a kiss and says: Zio! zio! ("uncle" in Italian), she looks like a big doll, she takes after Marilyn, who has put on a cool thirty pounds, she kisses me on both cheeks and says: You've gotten so thin! Michael comes out of their room pulling up his suspenders. He's put on at least fifty pounds and grown a dirty blond mustache down to his chin, he's lost all the hair on top of his head, the rest of it drapes down to his shoulders. His face is relaxed, smiley. I give him a kiss on each side of his mustache. He stinks of lavender cologne. He goes back to their room for the bottle of Italian brandy they brought me as a gift from Rome, we all sit down on my bed. The little one has to pee, she's screaming. They sit her down on my bidet, she takes a dump. Michael goes back to their room for some fresh diapers, and now she wants her bottle, which needs to be heated up, Michael heads down to the kitchen. Marilyn takes the opportunity to ask me: Isn't she adorable? The kid's howling because she doesn't want anyone to wipe her ass, which is all red, she got an infection at the beach in Rome. They powder her up, now she's puking on my sheets. She's all restless from the trip, plane rides make her sick. Michael arrives with the bottle, she doesn't want it, she starts crying. Marilyn shakes her, that seems to calm her down. She looks at me, she squints, she smiles at me. She wants me to hold her in my arms: Zio, she says. I take her. She knows how to sing, Michael says. This is quite clearly untrue. This kid's abnormal, she's three and still can't go to the bathroom on her own, she flops down in my arms like dead weight, her arms dangling. I lay her down on the bed, she starts howling: Zio! zio! I have to hold her. Fine, oh well, I sit on the bed with her on my lap. Marilyn tells me that Pierina will have her first communion soon, she's already bought her a dress. She has triple citizenship, French from her mom, American from her dad, Italian by birth. When she's an adult she'll be able to choose which one suits her best. Before they start asking me questions, I break in: what have you all been up to lately? Living the same old life in Rome. Going back and forth between Piazza Santa Maria and Piazza del Popolo, just waiting around for something to happen, the last thing was Fellini filming *Roma*, in which Marilyn landed a small role, although her scenes got cut out during edits. Michael doesn't do sculpture anymore, polyester cubes have gotten too expensive, he sells ties in a shop across from the Fontana di Trevi. They're happy, living in a small apartment in the suburbs, they're busy raising Pierina. Pierina is trying to stick her hand in my mouth, they think it's hilarious. She smells like shit, I try to get rid of her, to hand her over to Michael. She wants to stay with me. I have an urgent meeting, I say, I've got to run.

They're a little confused, they figured we'd go have dinner with the rugrat at the Italian place next door. But why? What do we even have to talk about anymore? Ever since Pietro died these idiots avoid talking about him, and that's the only subject we could possibly have in common. If I wanted to hear gossip about Rome I'd rather just walk around Paris, I hand them their daughter, say goodbye, and slam the door behind me. I go cruising at the last interesting pissoir left in the neighborhood, on Place Saint-Sulpice. No one's there, oh well, I unbutton my pants and wait, maybe someone will have the same idea as me. The cop on duty at the station goose steps across the street, eyes me severely, coughs, pisses half a gallon. I pretend not to notice him, he starts jerking off. I sneak a peek at his cock, it's not a cock, it's an eggplant! Are you kidding me! Harlot! I shout, and walk out, buttoning back up. I take a taxi, I go to Le César on Rue Chabannais, at least I won't run into any flame dames there, the owners are a lesbian couple. Dominique, the dumpy one, kisses me on both cheeks, we haven't seen each other for years. Claude shakes my hand. There are a lot of people upstairs. So, do you still live on Saint-Germain? They came to my house ten years ago for cocktails back in the days of our little tranny society, they still have their enchanting memories of it. I tell them that one of these days I'll throw another party, I don't want to spoil their illusion that time passes outside their bar just as it does inside, this illusion gives them the hope of retirement, they're thinking of marrying an old gay couple from the Arcadie group that's been courting them for a while now, they'll pool their four pensions and spend their days raising pheasants to hunt in the Gâtinais. I order a screwdriver and walk upstairs, it's full of smoke, covered in panther skins and aluminum. Everyone's dancing the java, I join in no problem, there's a queen who's older than me, one side of her body is paralyzed, and she still has a few moves. I grab a little Spaniard by the hips, he wants to lead me in a paso doble, I can't keep up, he goes off with another one who's just as old as me but wearing a tortoiseshell peineta in her blond curls for the occasion. All the younger men are lusting after her, it's annoying. Finally, the slow dance, I hurry and ask the little Spaniard for a dance, he's so short he only makes it up to my waist, he smells, he's been dancing since five p.m. and is waiting for the first Sunday morning metro to go back to the staff house where he lives in Neuilly, he's the servant of some rich folks, they only let him go out on Saturday night. I invite him for a glass of eau de vie at the hotel, he seems like the proper type. He's with a friend, a queen from his hometown outside Salamanca. Shouldn't be a problem, I invite both. Both? This freaks her out, she takes me for a pervert, she's looking for a pure love. I ask another one to dance, she says no. Around here, as soon as someone turns you down, everyone does, I ask two French queens, an Italian, a Yugoslav, one from Portugal and two from Spain, they all turn me down, they're looking for love. What for? So they can work for a husband instead of a boss. Their workload is reduced to fucking him punctually and chastely in the ass once a week, but they'll never be happy with the pay the old queen (in this case, that would be me) gives them, they seek out a second without leaving the first, which they keep around by starving him of cock, they want luxury, they're always unsatisfied and come here every Saturday in search of a new daddy, I just don't fit their profile. They want the kind of old poof that will buy them everything they see in *Le Nouvel Observateur*, *L'Express*, *Paris-Match*, *Jours de France*, which they flip through at their bosses'. They're disappointed when the daddy on offer isn't normal, but who is? If you want a rich daddy you have to go to Nice, Marbella, New York. And on top of that you have to be young and muscular, have a big cock, give in to all the old man's caprices, enemas in the middle of the night before fucking his ass, caring for him and his achy joints all day, taking the car out to pick up the old man's family members (the families think they're just chauffeurs, they work twice as much as regular servants, but they make ten times more, though how many make it that far?) who give them little tips and suspect they're potential criminals. A short Italian guy comes over and asks me to dance, a veritable dwarf but well built. We dance to "Warum, Warum," he hardly makes it up to my bellybutton, I keep one hand on his shoulder and stroke his neck with the other. He's tender and kind, I can feel his cock around the height of my knee, it must be pretty voluminous. He says he'd love to go home with me, she fucks ass, that's her specialty. Her name's Americo, wow, that's not a name you hear every day, I had an Italian uncle named Americo, he emigrated to South America and died of nostalgia. This Americo seems like an emigrant, too, he tends bar on a stool at an Italian place, he sends half his pay to his mom and three sisters of normal size in Calabria. The guy's horny as hell, says he hasn't had sex in three months, that it's hard for a dwarf, most people who get turned on by the idea of him are afraid of the ridicule and the ones who don't mind are usually perverts who want to roleplay as his mother, the ones from the pissoirs just want to piss on him. As for me, I couldn't care less that he's a dwarf, that doesn't besmirch the virtues of a fine Calabrese sausage. We call a radio-taxi, he hops up on a chair and helps me put on my jacket, you can tell he works at a restaurant. In the taxi he tries to stick his hand in my pants and touch my ass, I touch his cock. Yikes, it's enormous! I've never seen anything like it before, it's practically as thick as my stump, easily the size of a fist. I wonder if I'll be able to take it, I'm not particularly interested in going to Hôtel-Dieu at 5 a.m. to get stitches on my anus. At the same time, though, it turns me on like crazy. Did I remember to buy lube? I did. We pull up to Hôtel Crystal, the receptionist leans over the desk to have a look at both of us, and hands me a letter. It's Marilyn's handwriting. "We're leaving Pierina with you. We know you'll make a great godfather." I grab my key and we go up to the room. The girl's fast asleep on my bed, sucking her thumb. You like girls? I ask Americo. Want to fuck her ass at the same time? What's going through his mind? I need to convince him that it's normal. I bought her off her mom, she's a puttana, I fuck her ass every day, she'll be able to take his cock no problem. I take Pierina out of bed, she wakes up and asks for mommy, I take her clothes off, she's smaller than I thought, almost a baby. I lube up her behind and she starts crying. Americo takes out his cock and tries to shove it in.

To keep from making a mess in the bedroom we go to the bathroom. He starts to shove it in, Pierina howls, I cover her mouth and nostrils with my hand, she goes completely red. Americo shoves it in further and further, blood starts flowing, I choke Pierina, she turns violet, her body contorts, Americo howls with pleasure, and, just like that, he's done. We stick Pierina in the bidet and take a shower. I tell him to leave, he leaves. It's six a.m. I have time to add an extra chapter to my novel before eleven (eleven's when I have my meeting with my editor), I take out my last notebook and pen, roll myself a fat joint and start writing. I write at a clip until ten thirty, and just like that, the book's done. I dress little Pierina, walk downstairs with her in my arms, I ask the receptionist for the bill, I ask him to hold Pierina while I sign the check. He hands her back to me, we say see you around, I head off toward my editor's on Rue Garancière. I drop by the pissoir at Place Saint-Sulpice, someone's inside, I wait for him to finish, dump Pierina in the urinal, and go on my way. I added a final chapter, I tell my editor. Even better, now it'll be a 200-pager. He rubs his hands, offers me a cigar. You sure do write fast, he says. A novel in a week! That's right, I started just a week ago. What am I going to do now? I don't know, I'll get back into drawing, maybe write another play. With the five thousand francs he hands me I'll go take a load off in Rome for a week, I feel like wandering around. I call Marielle to see if I can come pick up the suitcase I left at hers. Come have one last Vouvray in Paris, she says. I thank my editor and walk out to the street. The police have taped off Place Saint-Sulpice, someone just raped and strangled a little girl in the public urinal, right under their noses. I take a taxi that drops me off at Marielle's place. Look at me, taking all these taxis! Thankfully, you have to walk everywhere in Rome, but walking in Paris has become such a drag. At least you can read the paper in a taxi. I'm sorry for how I acted two days ago, I tell Marielle. I left without waking her up. No, she's the one who's sorry, she doesn't know how she could have fallen asleep like that, when she woke up she listened to the tape, she had a great time with it. So you're off to Rome? Just for a few days. We make a date to meet at the Flore a week from Thursday, we'll have lunch at Lipp. We give each other a kiss on both cheeks, I grab my suitcase, I go.

Paris, October 16, 1976

Translator's Note

When I first read Copi, I felt a new emotion. I was at once buoyed up by his hilarity, charmed by his extravagance, caught off guard by his frankness, moved by his tenderness, and even, at times, frightened by his violence. It struck me that Copi wrote with a truly unique mixture of feelings. He was genuinely sentimental without ceding to the maudlin; surreal without hiding out in obscurity; hilarious without being superficial; cruel without fear of transgression; and somehow—this is the magic to his formula—he manages to remain consistently entertaining, if not straight out fun, throughout. He mixes such a particular cocktail of emotions that I'd say we wouldn't be jumping the gun if we just went ahead and coined the adjective "Copiesque" already.

In his 2000 talk "Exiles," given at the Austrian Society for Literature in Vienna, Roberto Bolaño cites Copi as an exemplar of those Argentine writers who expatriate and adopt "the languages of their new places of residence so naturally that we wonder if we aren't dealing with aliens rather than Argentines." And while, to be sure, the Argentine Copi did "pull a Beckett" and write the lion's share of his work in his second language of French—having swapped the Río de la Plata for the Seine in his early twenties—it would be misleading to say he allowed French to overwrite his Spanish-language origins. Rather, his French was always notoriously marked by his native Spanish.

The original French of *The Queen's Ball*, for example, is constellated with Spanish expressions and turns of phrase that have French acting in all sorts of funny ways, a point discussed in greater depth by Thibaud Croisy in his afterword, which follows this note. But to name my favorite example: he refers to Pierre's "Adam's nut (*noix*)," as per Spanish's *nuez de Adán*, rather than his "Adam's apple (*pomme*)," as one would say it in French. Given that it would not be *entirely* inconceivable, in the context of this book, for the narrator to dangle a Biblical testicle from his lover's throat, I decided to take the safe route and translate the phrase with English's conventional "Adam's apple." Because while these idiosyncrasies feel sincere and even charming in Copi's original French, I found that their deliberate reproductions often felt stilted, if not outright confusing, in English translation. Perhaps Spanish and French, sharing so much DNA, simply allow for such fusion, while English, though profoundly influenced by Romance languages, lies too far afield for such moments to feel anything but as out of place as "a fish on a tree."

Especially since this is the first work of Copi's prose to appear in English, I decided to turn my focus toward other aspects of his style that wouldn't lead to a translation-induced misunderstanding that Copi was a "difficult" writer, since his books, even with their avant-garde qualities, are hard to put down. To name a few: his serpentine run-ons, the velocity of his narrative gallop, mid-sentence tense shifts, and his electrifying tendency to switch a character's pronouns suddenly from *he* to *she* and back again in the same scene.

The original French of *The Queens' Ball* also sparkles

with phrases in English and Italian, which are sometimes contorted for the sake of play, but which, at times, are simply incorrect in terms of grammar. Consulting with Copi's brother, Federico Botana, who suggested that these qualities were likely not deliberate, I decided to take the following approach: if a mistake contributed to a character's personality—for example, it's classic Marilyn to insist on speaking English even though she is practically incapable of expressing herself in it—then it stands. If it doesn't serve such a purpose, however, I corrected it in order to avoid unhelpful confusion.

Another distinct, though potentially curious, aspect of the translation is that it maintains the French (and, for that matter, Spanish) term *travesti*, rather than using the possible English-language correlate of "transvestite." This one took some thinking. While "transvestite" here would have invoked the image of a "man" dressing up in "women's clothing," thereby binding Copi's characters to a rigid gender binary and leaving no question about the fact that the characters in discussion were essentially "men" at the end of the day, *travesti* allows the reader to engage them on a vaster, less deterministic field of gender fluidity.

While reading *The Queen's Ball*, it's hard to avoid the feeling that we're reading a visionary novel from recent years. We have to keep in mind, however, that it was in fact written half a century ago, in the 1970s, and the very possibilities of sex and gender expression in the world itself were different. (For this same reason, the translation omits more recent terms such as "trans" and "queer.") In the case of Copi's travestis, it felt truer to use the very term they would have used to describe themselves, a term which ultimately allows his readers to appreciate the diversity of their self-expression and embodiment. It feels important, as well, to note that while the French verb *se travestir* does refers to crossdressing, it also pertains to general acts of disguise and more festive gestures, such as an actor dressing up as what he is not, or a party-goer preparing for a masked ball.

That said, I am by no means the first translator to maintain *travesti* in recent times, and would like to signal two points of inspiration behind this choice: Shook's 2023 translation of Mario Bellatin's *Kawabata, the Writer, the Travesti Philosopher, and the Fish*, and Kit Maude's 2022 translation of Camila Sosa Villada's *Bad Girls*, the informative preface to which dives into the Argentine Sosa Villada's own engagement with the term—a text which informed my decision here, too.

In closing, I'd like to thank a few people who were instrumental to this book: Federico Botana, who kindly granted us permission to go ahead with this project and wove some top-notch yarns about Copi in our correspondence; Thibaud Croisy, Copi's current editor in France, who worked with us closely and allowed us to use his own brilliant critical apparatus from the 2021 Christian Bourgois edition of *Le Bal des folles*, revised for this edition; Yasmine Seale, who read this translation word for word against the French, offering countless lifesaving edits that now define the translation and sharpen Copi's *folle* sense of humor in English; Olivia Baes, who saved our ship with swift translation work; Chris Wait, who shared enthusiasm for Copi early on; Adrian de Banville, who solved the mystery of a scene; Francesco Pedraglio, who revised the Italian; Gia Gonzales, who shone a light on several aspects of formatting; and, of course, Mitch Anzuoni, who not only took on this book that flies in the face of so many prevailing conventions, but even sent me pictures of several of the hotels in Paris where some its grisliest scenes take place.

KIT SCHLUTER

A Queen in Wonderland

Afterword by Thibaud Croisy

The novel is not only mobile, it is moving, it transforms as it develops, it knows not what it must become. The nature of the novel is infinity. The novel is an autobiography in action. The novelist is his own creature. He says "I" to lie. The self no longer exists. He declares himself man and woman, head and stomach, child and elder. He dies as many times as it takes. He loves without ever tiring. The nature of the novel is sex. The novel is a sexual act.[1]

—PIERRE BOURGEADE

Reissued in 2020, *Warum*, Pierre Bourgeade's novel, would undoubtedly have delighted Copi. It traces the bohemian life of Pierre, the author's double, and his adventures with women, notably a young German woman whose nickname alone captures the mystery of love: Warum ("Why?"). Written more than twenty years apart by two novelists who were also playwrights, *The Queens' Ball* (1977) and *Warum* (1999) belong to the category of books which are danced, picaresque tales in the form of rounds where loose narrators jump from

_____

1. Pierre Bourgeade, *Warum* (Auch: éditions Tristram, 2020), 21.

one partner to the next, one country to the next, and whose sex, age, and moods are transformed with the snap of a finger. The two novels are carnivals of fictions, narrative orgies, improvisations in action where multiple stories intertwine, fecundate, and proliferate *ad infinitum*.

On the back cover of *Warum*, the publishers recall how Pierre Bourgeade's book was highly praised upon its release. "Everyone agreed that this splendidly written novel of rare shamelessness was truly the work of a master. But perhaps it was too much, too soon. Twenty years on—and at a time when all moral standards have been revised—*Warum* seems even more transgressive. Will a new generation be able to grasp it?"[1] they ask themselves in a non-rhetorical question which suggests that this will be no easy feat. The same could be said of Copi's *The Queens' Ball*, a monstrous party which, culminating in a climax of dark humor, can perhaps unsettle our times even more than it did his own. Copi had warned us, however. "No cops" here, and so "no punishments."[2] Instead, a censor-free voyage to the mad depths of a queen's imagination.

After a long history of pussyfooting around homosexuality—beginning with his first play, *Lamento por el ángel* (Lamento for the angel) (1961)—Copi lanced the boil in Paris with *L'Homosexuel ou la difficulté de s'exprimer*[3] (1971), a painful, outlandish comedy which also served as his

---

1. Sylvie Martigny and Jean-Hubert Gailliot in Bourgeade, *Warum*, cover text.
2. Copi, *The Queens' Ball*, trans. Kit Schluter (New York: Inpatient Press, 2024), 13.
3. One of the scarce few works by Copi that exist in English, this play was translated by one Anni Lee Taylor into English in the 1970s under the clever title of *The Homosexual or the Difficulty of Sexpressing Oneself*. See Copi, *Plays, Vol. 1* (London: Calder Publications, 1976).—Ed.

theatrical coming-out. From then on, the young Argentinian would live "publicly as a homosexual, after hiding it almost entirely for a long time,"[1] as he himself put it. And if he had previously been noted for his taciturn homosexual characters (Alfredo, Irina[2]), with *The Queens' Ball*, he took advantage of the maelstrom of the "sexual revolution" to inaugurate a new poetics of delirium. The cornerstone of this new edifice was *Loretta Strong* (1974), the monologue of a cosmonaut lost in space, whose logorrheic speech desperately seeks to fill the void. "Hello, hello, can you hear me?"[3] By incarnating the adrift earthling on stage, Copi adopted the persona of a travesti and queen—two archetypes with whom he would long remain affiliated in the French imagination, though they would overshadow the more melancholic aspects of his work. In any case, it was during this period that *The Queens' Ball* sprung into existence. In the spring of 1976, Copi was on tour in the United States. He had just played *Loretta Strong* in Baltimore, where he broke his leg after a bad fall (and not because of a boa constrictor!), and then at La Mama in New York. Temporarily incapacitated, he began writing this book, his second novel, at the Chelsea Hotel, where he stayed with his photographer friend Martine Barrat, then in New Hampshire, while staying with his Argentinian compatriot Julian Cairol. In a sense, *The Ball* can be read as a sort of narrative variation of his solo play, or its prolongation, which reconstructed, from a distance, a fantasized Paris in which he had regained full mobility. For if *Loretta*'s score resembles

---

1. Copi, *The Queens' Ball*, trans. Schluter, 13.
2. Shown ten years apart, *Lamento por el ángel* and *L'Homosexuel ou la difficulté de s'exprimer* respectively feature Alfredo and Irina, two characters who refuse to put their sexuality into words.
3. Copi, *Loretta Strong* (Paris: Christian Bourgois éditeur, 1999), 126.

material Copi had written for himself (and around which he happily embroidered), *The Queens' Ball* propagates folly without any intermediaries, in a theatrical novel the author plays out on the stage of our imagination.

The French title of Copi's novel is *Le Bal des folles*, or *The Ball of the* Folles. The translation has used "queen" as translation of this central term. But what does "*folle*" mean, anyway? And how can we summarize this twirling figure who has eluded all attempts at a definition? The French term, literally the feminine adjective for "crazy," originally designates a woman who displays disturbing behavioral tendencies because of her altered mental faculties. It is only by extension, and evidently in a pejorative manner, that heterosexuals began to use this term to describe so-called "inverts," effeminate homosexuals who suffered from "sexual inversion." Growing up at a time when homosexuality was still considered "deviant," Copi was undeniably aware of the polysemy of the word *folle*, which also existed in Spanish as *locas*, thus marking a point of contact between his two languages.[1] Moreover, when he moved to Paris from Argentina in 1962, he began to frequent gay hangouts (Madame Arthur, Le Carrousel, Le Pimm's, Le Fiacre, La Pergola...) where he discovered an entire swarm of *folles* who were reappropriating its stigma by performing it, upending it, and ironically transforming its "pathology" into a flamboyant lifestyle. Descendants of the turn-of-the-century

---

1. English does not share this coincidence by which a feminine word meaning "crazy" can be used to refer to a homosexual or effeminate man. Given its shared valences with *folle*, "queen" seems to be English's nearest equivalent: not only can "queen" be used both pejoratively and positively to refer to an extravagant gay man, but it also overtly invokes an image of high femininity.—Ed.

"*tantes*"[1] (literally "aunts" in English), these uninhibited *folles* played at reversing norms as frivolously as possible, without any justification, and even if they were not always transvestites (at times keeping their masculine appearances), they dragged the world through the performative power of their words, feminizing wildly, and alternating between genders at the whim of their caprices or (false) foolishness.[2] From then on, *folle* was less an immutable quality than it was a state of mind, a manner of seeing and speaking, one which could potentially even be adopted by heterosexuals.[3]

Better still, playing the *folle* (pretending to be what others wished you to be) allowed you to claim that you belonged to another minority (that of women), while simultaneously mocking this wish, which you knew was impossible (or could only take place in the imagination, through a tacit agreement between both parties). In this respect, and as Guy Hocquenghem points out, the *folle* has nothing to do with

1. In French, the words *tante* (fairy) and *tapette* (pansy) were used pejoratively, beginning in the 19th century, to refer to an effeminate homosexual man defined less by his desire or his sexual practices than by the "sexualized character" he played in public.

2. Copi is renowned for alternating between the feminine and masculine forms of the subject, even within the same sentence, which can give rise to some surprising images. This is the case with Americo, for example ("He says he'd love to go home with me, she fucks ass, that's her specialty") and with the *folles* at the baths ("I watch a queen swimming through it, he's screaming and grasping at the railing [...] she's already dead"). This device is also a literary illustration of the "third sex" with which *folles* are sometimes associated, i.e. an in-between sex combining both masculine and feminine characteristics.

3. For Patrick Cardon, there is such a thing as the "hetero-*folle*." He claims that "a whole encyclopedia on the *folle* could be made, [...] one which would have nothing to do with sex, sexuality, or sexual orientation." See Patrick Cardon, "Précis de follosophie" (Manual of *folle*-osophy), in Michel Cressole, *Une folle à sa fenêtre* (A *folle* at her window) (Lille: éditions GayKitschCamp, 1996), 7-8.

those "more truthful roles, more suited to simple sexologi-
cal truths: liberated homosexuals sporting moustaches and
aftershave, successful transsexuals, or the young community's
bisexuals…"[1] On the contrary, the *folle* is a figure belonging
to inadequacy, discrepancy, and playacting—she is theatrical by nature. Because beneath her scatterbrained pussycat
or silly goose exterior, the *folle* is not so senseless. She is
aware that the woman does not exist within and of herself,
plays at being one herself (to please, dupe, cheat, or love the
man), and by chasing this idealized image of the woman,
she surrenders to being a double pretender, a derisory actress
who only picks the most sublime roles for herself (the "diva,"
the "lady," the "woman of the world"[2]) and perhaps winds up
being sublime by virtue of being derisory. Long before the
emergence of *gender studies*, the *folle* is a "counter-identity"[3]
revealing the hazy roles that everyone plays (for themselves)
(the illustrious succession of "trips" that summarize Pierre's
life: the "queen trip," the "hippie trip," the "artist trip," the
"religious trip," etc.).

Contaminated by the folly of the time, *The Ball* features

1. Guy Hocquenghem, "Invitation au délire" (Invitation to delirium), in
La Dérive homosexuelle (The homosexual drift) (Paris: Jean-Pierre Delarge
éditeur, 1977), 144. In the eyes of Copi and Guy Hocquenghem, medical
progress was not yet sufficiently developed for the "travesti" to become
a woman in 1977. "It will be ten years before there are any convincing
travestis in France," the narrator says, "but it's crucial, I'll say it again, to
make up your mind early." Copi, *The Queens' Ball*, trans. Schluter, 42.
2. An example is Madame in Jean Genet's *The Maids* (1947), a woman
which could have come from a *folle*'s imagination. Copi played this character in a production directed by Mario Missiroli, which premiered at
Turin's Teatro Stabile in 1980.
3. Cardon, "Précis de follosophie," 5. For further information on the *folle*,
see Jean-Yves Le Talec, *Folles de France. Repenser l'homosexualité masculine*
(*Folles* of France: rethinking masculine homosexuality) (Paris: éditions La
Découverte, 2008).

characters trapped in a gigantic "merry-go-round of appearances,"[1] all of whom are classified as different types of *folles*—or, as in the translation, queens: "boutique queens," "demented queens," "bourgeois queens," "ditsy queens," "fussy queens," "theater queens"… But its originality (and no doubt also its great tour de force) lies in the fact that such folly is not just a vision of the world. It is also a language—light, bouncy, sinuous, serpentine…[2] And all through his crazy novel, Copi manages to mimic the meanderings of this spewing discourse, to play all the roles, to speak all the languages ("il cinema porta disgrazia,"[3] "Warum, warum,"[4] "Go back to the fridge!"[5]), to imitate all the accents ("a nethcafé?," "an anithette?"[6]) and goes from cock to ass without any transitions or time-outs. As flamboyant as a Harlequin costume, the novel's voice in the original French pulverizes literary conventions (no quotation marks, no hyphens for dialogue) and hurls ahead with approximate syntax and Spanish-language turns of phrase which distort the French language, unhinging it, cracking it open, and transforming it into another language that is no longer quite French, but not quite Spanish either.[7] The novel gives us the illusion that it has been

1. I have borrowed this expression from Jean-Paul Sartre, who used it in reference to Genet's theater in *Saint-Genet, comédien et martyr* (Paris: Gallimard, Tel, 2011), 675; *Saint-Genet, Actor and Martyr*, trans. Bernard Frechtman (New York: George Braziller, 1963).
2. The motif of the sinuous line runs throughout the novel, from the hysterical convulsions of the *folles* to Pierina, by way of Marilyn's boa. The motif also applies to Copi's baroque, zigzagging sentences.
3. Copi, *The Queens' Ball*, trans. Schluter, 5.
4. *Ibid.*, 154.
5. *Ibid.*, 45.
6. *Ibid.*, 103.
7. Language "inversions," in which one word is used in place of another, are frequent. For example, the narrator says, "*Tu n'es pas* à l'épargne *des réalités de l'existence*," whereas one would expect, "*Tu n'es pas* à l'abri *des réalités de*

written "at a clip,"[1] that the words were thrown on paper in the exact order they arrived, with no later proofreading or editing (which is not true, as evidenced by the study of its manuscripts). *The Ball* seems to be that ideal book, the one every writer dreams of: the instantaneous transcription of a writer's stream of consciousness, an "organic" work which seems to have recorded itself on a "tape,"[2] inviting its readers to tune in to its pure, raw, and timeless imagination.

If Copi swapped the character of the "homosexual" for the *folle*, it was also because the streets of Paris had just staged a sudden explosion of folly. In March 1971, in the wake of May 1968 and the Stonewall riots (1969), lesbian feminists and "rebellious homosexuals"[3] formed the Front homosexuel d'action révolutionnaire (Homosexual Front for Revolutionary Action) (FHAR). Copi dallied with these organizations without ever truly belonging to them, for he was wary of militant groups, which often turned into "gangs" (he uses the metaphor in *La Guerre des pédés* (Fag wars), a sequel

---

l'existence." Hispanisms are also prevalent. Copi refers to Pierre's Adam's apple as his "noix *d'Adam* (Adam's *nut*)," which comes from Spanish's phrase *nuez de Adán* of the same meaning, where one would expect him to use French's "pomme *d'Adam* (Adam's *apple*)." Also, when the narrator says the wolf "*s'interne dans la mer*," he is constructing his sentence from the Spanish verb *internarse* ("to penetrate" or "to intern oneself"), which produces an effect of strangeness in French, as one never "interns oneself" in a liquid.
1. *Ibid.*, 156.
2. *Ibid.*, 148. According to the narrator, the last three chapters of the novel were written in "four notebooks" and recorded on "two tapes," using Marielle de Lesseps's tape player. This is pure invention. The manuscript of *The Ball* is in fact made up of eight notebooks and zero recordings.
3. FHAR, *Rapport contre la normalité* (Report against normality) (Montpellier: éditions GayKitschCamp, 2013), 43. Very quickly, lesbians began to break away from homosexuals, whom they deemed misogynistic, and set up their own movements, such as the Gouines Rouges.

or "rejoinder"[1] to *The Queens' Ball*). In Paris, at the École des Beaux-Arts amphitheater, FHAR members theorized the revolutionary dimension of homosexuality, where "the roles of man/woman, fucked/fucker, master/slave [...] were mutable and could be reversed at any time," in contrast to heterosexuality, which, they argued, implied the domination of man over woman. These provocative, utopian activists advocated for a "homosexual conception of the world" and invited "queers" to extend homosexuality's egalitarian experience to society as a whole. "We'll be normal when you're all homosexuals,"[2] declared Guy Hocquenghem, one of the movement's leading figures (and one of Copi's closest friends).

Unfortunately for them, these libertarian (and gladly libertine) activists were soon overtaken on the left by the Gazolines, a gang of *folles* from their own ranks, whose scent is found in Copi's novel. The Gazolines, whose most notable members included Hélène Hazera, Maud Molyneux, Jenny Bel'Air, and Paquita Paquin, represented "a kind of psychedelic homosexual Dadaism, a violently anti-authoritarian and derisive ideology."[3] Indeed, this little troupe spent its time mocking leftists, accusing them of homophobic undertones,[4] and mocking FHAR members who felt a little too

1. Copi, "La vie est un tango, *Che* Copi..." (Life is a tango, *che* Copi...), interview by Giovanni Monaco, *Gai Pied Hebdo*, no. 64 (April 9, 1983): 35.
2. FHAR, *Rapport contre la normalité*, 71-77.
3. Hélène Hazera quoted by Michael Sibalis in "L'arrivée de la libération gay en France. Le Front homosexuel d'action révolutionnaire" (The arrival of gay liberation in France. The Homosexual Front for Revolutionary Action), trans. Nathalie Paulme, in *Genre, culture & société*, "Révolution/Libération," no. 3 (Spring 2010). The Gazolines were originally called "Camping Gaz Girls" in reference to the tea they prepared on portable camping stoves during the FHAR general assemblies.
4. *À voix nue* (The naked voice), "Hélène Hazera, une femme de combat"

tempted by the spirit of seriousness, in order to prevent the movement's institutionalization. For the most part, the Gazolines were also "travestis"[1] or boys who did not quite know where they stood, but who stuck out because of their carnivalesque profile: their *camp* spirit, hyper-femininity, taste for cross-dressing, high-class snobbery, keen wit, and sense of criticism. Doped up on hormones and pumped up on films from the Cinémathèque, where they had set up their HQ, the Gazolines sowed a "pink" terror which is still remembered today. They pranced through the streets of the Latin Quarter in groups, showing off their outrageous get-ups (retro in style, wearing second-hand clothes from flea markets and necklaces with dildos instead of pearls), entering the Saint-Germain-des-Prés cafés to make their rallying cry heard ("Diiiiiiick!") and they marched with the workers on Labor Day to demand "champagne, coke, and

(Hélène Hazera, a Woman of Combat), aired August 29, 2017 on France Culture. "Leftist movements treated homosexuals like subhumans," recalls Hélène Hazera. "My friend Michel Cressole was a member of a Trotsky-ist movement in Clermont-Ferrand. One day, a worker needed housing. Michel offered to put him up, but someone in the group said, pointing at Michel, 'What if he makes a pass at him?' The group leader replied, 'Well, he'll just have to punch him in the face.' That same evening, Michel left."

1.   Here, I am adopting the novel's terminology. In the 1970s, the word "travesti" was still used in French to refer to men who lived as women (and who had not undergone surgery). They themselves used the term. Like a skilled playwright, Copi lumps all the characters who change their physical appearance and clothing together under the terms "travestis" and *folles*, emphasizing the theatricality of their approach and setting aside the gender issue (at most, he sometimes distinguishes between "travestis" and "real trannies"—an oxymoron for "transsexuals"). As Copi sees the world through the prism of performance, he thinks of the travesti ("real" or "fake") as an individual who wishes to change *roles*. A change that can vary *ad infinitum* since roles are obviously far more diverse than the sexes. "The *folle* is a homosexual with an abstract sexuality," adds Patrick Cardon.

frills."[1] The Gazolines were a guaranteed scandal. They were also regularly hounded by the police, who were eager to put an end to their outbursts. These were the Gazolines that Copi knew so well, the ones we encounter in the guise of a small "society of queens"[2] who "[down] feminine hormones by the fistful" and sell their newspaper "for its weight in gold at the queen clubs."[3] Their leader, Marilyn, was inspired by the real life Marie France, a "transsexual" cabaret performer who impersonated Marilyn Monroe at L'Alcazar and whom the Gazolines had crowned as their muse. A "foolish girl" who put on a "pathetic little number,"[4] notes the *Ball* narrator in yet another vicious remark.

If these odd birds had seduced Copi, it was perhaps because they embodied, in his eyes, the contemporary and paroxysmal versions of the *folle*: they were a kind of "super-*folle*," blurring the boundaries between art and life as they carnivalized the world, whereas transformists sensibly kept themselves to a small stage. Their exuberance was such that it also provided him with excellent dramatic and narrative

....

1. "Proletarians of all countries, stroke yourselves!" they also proclaimed, hijacking Marx and Engels' well-known injunction in the *Communist Manifesto* ("Proletarians of all countries, unite!"). This tendency to subvert political slogans revealed their Situationist influences.

2. Copi, *The Queens' Ball*, trans. Schluter, 35.

3. *Ibid.*, 28. We might hastily conclude that the Gazolines were the ancestors of today's *queers*. But this would be forgetting that the 1970s context has absolutely nothing to do with our own, given that the Gazolines were born to a society that penalized homosexuality and repressed cross-dressing. What's more, their group resembled less an established movement than it did a gathering of free spirits akin to a hoax or a parody.

4. *Ibid.*, 21, 73. Copi knew Marie France well. A singer and actress, she was approached to play the role of Daphné in Copi's *La Tour de la Défense* (Defense tower) (1981), before it was finally awarded to Bernadette Lafont. See Marie France, *Elle était une fois* (Once upon a dame) (Paris: Denoël, 2003).

material. Moreover, in the early 1970s, Copi was toying with the signs of his own femininity. He had let his hair grow down to his shoulders, took advantage of his slender figure to slip into women's costumes, played the role of Garbo in *L'Homosexuel* before taking on Loretta, and perhaps secretly admired (or pretended to admire?) the audacity of the Gazolines who had crossed the threshold of a total metamorphosis. "It's such a drag, spending the whole day as a target for comments like this from everyone, on the street, in public places," notes the narrator. "In fact, I think that Pierre and the rest of them are really courageous. Personally, I'm not a travesti because I'm not brave enough."[1] Nevertheless, by embroidering on the Gazolines, Copi satires them completely, stripping them of their political dimension and lumping them in with the masses of *folles*, reducing them to the rank of vulgar delinquents obsessed with drugs, sex, money, and tricks. They "stole their food in the supermarkets and their dresses in the Prisunic and the Marché aux Puces," "[worked] the sidewalk on Rue Sainte-Anne," caught an old man, tied him to the bed, and "[pissed] and shit on him and spit in his eyes."[2] Ultimately, Marilyn and the others are just another monstrosity in an open-air cesspool where everyone pretty much does what they want (which is, above all, absolute nonsense). This clearly illustrates Copi's ambivalent stance on folly and the *folle*. For, while he revels in it, glorifies it, and adopts it as his own, he also criticizes it by portraying

1. *Ibid.*, 31.
2. *Ibid.*, 23, 25. Estranged from their families, some Gazolines prostituted themselves, shoplifted, performed in cabarets, and lived in communes. François Jonquet chronicled the vagabond life of one such member, Jenny Bel'Air, who went on to become a transgender icon of Parisian nightlife. See *Jenny Bel'Air: une créature* (Jenny Bel'Air: a creature) (Paris: éditions Pauvert, 2001).

it as an empty craze that everyone is adopting in an attempt to exist and indulge their most vile instincts.

Written by a "special" *folle*—unique and critical—the novel still leaves us with the impression that folly can wear thin over time, as if the distinguishing characteristics of its "outsiders" were doomed to inevitable ruin. In the backdrop, the book's title conjures up two rituals of folly which place the moment's epiphenomenon into perspective. The first is the famous "Bal des folles,"[1] which was held at the Salpêtrière Hospital in Paris in the 1880s. To celebrate Carnival, the nursing staff organized an unprecedented encounter between "hysterics" and carefully selected representatives of the outside world. The evening was thought to entertain the patients, who were allowed to dress up as gypsies, Colombines, magicians, bandits, musketeers, Zouaves, and Pierrots, while high society slummed it to cringe at the patients' impressive contortions. It was a double spectacle.[2] A few decades later, during the interwar period, a new "Bal des folles" took over, featuring another category of "deviants." Twice a year, on the eve of Mardi Gras and mid-Lent, hundreds of transvestites flocked to the gates of the former Magic-City amusement park beside the Eiffel Tower. As in a fairy tale, the "Parisian Tout-Tata"[3] suddenly sprang from its hiding hole and

1. While Copi used this name for the title of his novel, the English translation of this historical event is literally "The Mad Women's Ball." The pun is a victim of translation.—Ed.

2. See "Le Bal des folles" in *Le Petit Parisien*, no. 3794 (March 19, 1887): 2, and Virginie Bloch-Lainé's radio documentary directed by Clotilde Pivin: *Le Bal des folles de la Salpêtrière* (The ball of Salpêtrière Hospital's mad women), aired February 15-16, 2020 on France Culture.

3. Here, "Tout-Tata" is composed of the word "Tout," which signifies "All," and the diminutive for "Tante," or "Tata." Period document cited by Farid Chenoune in "Leur bal. Notes sur des photos de Magic-City, bal des

paraded in plain sight. The halls of the abandoned park were invaded by mobs of chambermaids, matrons, feathered duchesses, fat Gretchens with blond pigtails, and other celebrity look-alikes—such as "Marlene," "Mae West," or "Garbo," who would have made the derisory Marilyn shudder with their grotesque, botch-job costumes... At one o'clock in the morning, when the party was in full swing, the most beautiful *folles* were invited to cross the "transvestite bridge" for a chance to win the catwalk-competition, which was judged by a jury of the (heterosexual) stars of the moment: Raimu, Michel Simon, Joséphine Baker, and Mistinguett—the famed music-hall queen who would later be interpreted by a 1970s transvestite, La Grande Eugène... Transgressive and sulphureous, the masked ball was a singular event, for in its context of mainstream crossdressing, "sexual inversion" became the norm, as heterosexuals were banished to the margins (though they were, of course, the ones who judged the *folles* and awarded them prizes).

In the 1970s, as if folly were making a cyclical comeback, minorities resurrected the spirit of the Roaring Twenties (a period in French known as "*Les Années folles*"). Their festivities

tantes de l'entre-deux-guerres" (Their ball. Notes on photos of Magic-City, the ball of interwar-period '*tantes*'), in *Modes pratiques, revue d'histoire du vêtement et de la mode*, no. 1 (November 2015): 248-285. Photos of Magic-City's "bal des folles" can be seen in Brassaï's *Le Paris secret des années trente*, known in English as *The Secret Paris of the '30s* (1976). Moreover, it's important to note that the Parisian drag balls, of which Magic-City was the emblem, had their New York counterparts well into the 1930s. According to George Chauncey, these festivities were "the most important collective events in gay society," with some people looking forward to them all year. They sometimes attracted thousands of people, including heterosexuals who would rent upper lodges to watch the transvestites on the dance floors. See George Chauncey, *Gay New York: Gender, Urban Culture, and the Making of the Gay Male World, 1890-1940* (New York: Basic Books, 1994).

were held in balls, clubs, and above all in a discotheque located in a former theater: the legendary Palace, which hosted a themed evening entitled "Magic-City Ball". Yves Saint Laurent, Karl Lagerfeld, Thierry Mugler and Helmut Newton were among its attendants. Meanwhile, a Gazoline named Hélène Hazera also yielded to the nostalgic trend by seeking out a collection of decadent novels by Charles Étienne, a "sub-writer"[1] who had chronicled transvestite balls, and to whom we owe a certain... *Bal des folles* (1930). According to Hélène Hazera, it was this "old tat" that inspired the title of Copi's novel. And so, when one of his chapters is entirely dedicated to a ball with cotillion and lobster hats, it is impossible to miss the allusion to the mythical festivities of homosexual culture. Except that Copi's ball is deceptive: it takes place in an underground structure, a universal space (a sauna where everyone looks alike), and gets interrupted by the arrival of a gang of "real trannies"[2] (reminiscent of Marilyn's gang) and the narrator's criminal adjustment of the thermostat that puts an end to the masquerade. Here, again, Copi nurtures paradox: on the one hand, the thermostat attack annihilates synthetic folly and wrecks the ghetto

---

1. "At the flea market, Michel Cressole and I collected books by a sub-writer called Charles Étienne," recalls Hélène Hazera. "We found a strange novel, *Le Bal des folles*, with thirty pages describing the mid-Lent ball in Magic-City. Copi stumbled across it and it became *The Queens' Ball*. Copi recycled everything." Hélène Hazera, interview by Isabelle Barbéris, in Barbéris, "Copi: le texte et la scène" (Copi: the text and the scene), (PhD thesis, Université Paris Nanterre, 2007), 552. For a description of the Magic-City ball, see Charles Étienne, *Le Bal des folles* (Paris: éditions Curio, 1930), 152-170.
2. Copi, *The Queens' Ball*, trans. Schluter, 124. Marilyn's identity is unstable over the course of the book. In the beginning, she is less a "woman" than she is a "fag hag," a "virgin" constantly insinuating herself into the queens' world by "acting like one of them." In the end, Michael's "tiny cock" gets the better of this virginity of hers and she becomes a mother.

of those circling the pool; on the other, it brings that same folly to the surface as to disseminate it, as it is proliferated in a perhaps even more malignant form. A good crank, and the novel takes off again…

Dancing a ball is always about conjuring lost time, recalling some original impulse and reliving the insouciance of youth, even if we are all fully aware that life is leading us further away from it daily. Pierre Bourgeade perfectly captures this melancholy of bodies in the ball he imagined for *Warum*, an event in which guests are required to wear masks mimicking "the features they had at the most darling moment of their adolescence—their choice!—but between the ages of twelve and sixteen, naturally."[1] Once the dance is over, the narrator is struck by yet another reminder of the fleeting nature of time. He is reunited with Éva, his former mistress, only to find that her once beautiful eyes are now of a milky white and as extinguished as dead stars. A morbid, sickening image that makes him realize an entire lifetime has passed in an instant, without him even noticing. The shock is so great that he races to his desk as to write a book and "pour [his] youth, [his] desire, [his] strength into it", convinced that "survival"[2] is the "true nature of the novel" and that this genre is the only way to cheat death a few steps.

While it may not be obvious upon first reading *The Ball*, a similar sentiment underlies the whole fiction, though here external events are not what plunge the narrator into melancholy. On the contrary, he himself lets the emotion come, take hold, invade him, because melancholy is already inscribed in

1. Bourgeade, *Warum*, 206.
2. *Ibid.*, 239.

him like some primal mood he can never quite shake off. In the first chapter of *The Ball*, the writer vegetates, does not write, loses his manuscripts. But as he wanders through the streets of Paris, he thinks again of Pierre, who really does exist ("he's my friend in real life")[1] and this thought brings back "the memory of Pierre's smell," then "the image of Pierre's corpse."[2] "And the novel writes itself in the pain his death causes [him]."[3] At this point, one might be tempted to think that the story is autobiographical or an autofiction. The narrator's identity seems to coincide with the author ("that's my real name, my name is Raoul Damonte but I sign my books with Copi,"[4] "I'm still drawing comics for the papers, I've written and staged a few plays")[5] and the publisher's character, whose offices are on Rue Garancière, closely resembles Christian Bourgois, the book's "real" publisher. And yet, as memories flood the book's pages, the imagination kicks in, seizing memory as to draw upon it to fill the original void. Which was to be expected, as memory is already an imaginary reconstruction, a fiction in the making—which is why, for Copi, autobiographical truth can never exist. For Copi, writing is always a lie, a "mixture of dream and reality"[6] in which we can no longer distinguish truth from

---

1. Copi, *The Queens' Ball*, trans. Schluter, 4.
2. *Ibid.*, 8.
3. *Ibid.*, 4.
4. *Ibid.*, 39. One detail nevertheless catches our attention: "Raoul" is the French version of Copi's actual first name, Raúl, a linguistic double that alters, transposes, and reinvents his real first name.
5. *Ibid.*, 46.
6. *Ibid.*, 128. Copi defines this poetics as early as his first play, *Lamento por el ángel*, in which one of his characters asserts that "imagination [...] mingles with memory and surpasses it." See Copi, *Lamento pour un ange*, trans. Laurey Braguier and Thibaud Croisy (Paris: Christian Bourgois éditeur, 2024).

falsehood, nor know what is memory or fantasy, and in what proportions. The advantage of such confusion is that writing is never backward-looking, since imagination revives worlds that are lost to the present and prolongs them, while also liquidating them as best as possible. In this sense, *The Queens' Ball* is indeed "a crime novel" with "two guilty parties"[1]: the writer, the serial killer who shreds his memorial and imaginary visions the moment they appear; and the reader, who delights in watching the author wade through the bloodbath of writing in an attempt to overcome himself...

Fortunately, the momentum sometimes comes to a halt. The folly takes a beat. And Copi is reunited with Marielle, the only "real" woman in the book. A charming sphinx observing the ball from a fixed point in the distance, who permits it to happen and ensures it can go on (hence the dedication to the woman without whom the party would not exist[2]). A bohemian artist and young woman from a good family, Marielle is a kind of inverted double of the narrator: like him, she tries to write, but fails to do so, incapable of entering the state of folly that sparks the novel. Perhaps she does not want it, does not need it. Perhaps she also has a more peaceful relationship with her own void, one which allows her to content herself with the simple things: dinner at Ping-Pong, a good bottle of Vouvray, a cigarette while listening to her friend's outrageous stories, as the good spectator she is. The narrator knows that he will join her one day, and this is precisely what happens when the spell nears its conclusion. In the final chapter, in the early hours of the morning, Copi opens the door of the César and the atmosphere has changed.

1. Copi, *The Queens' Ball*, trans. Schluter, 13.
2. In "real life," Marielle de Lesseps was a friend of Copi's. See Notes, 190-191.

Claude and Dominique, the owners, are preparing for their retirement and going to leave Paris. Upstairs, the dance floor looks more like a court of miracles than a select dance hall: the *folles* have all aged. One is a hemiplegic; the other is a dwarf who "hasn't had sex in three months."[1] Copi himself is having a hard time finding a partner ("I ask two French queens, an Italian, a Yugoslav, one from Portugal and two from Spain, they all turn me down")[2] and when he returns home with Americo, the only queen who has deigned to follow him, the handsome Pierre and his divine bellybutton have shriveled into little Pierina, a horrible brat who "turns violet"[3] when we she gets impaled. As for Marilyn, she is not any better off. She ends the ball on the floor, washed out, as an Italian *mamma* "who has put on a cool thirty pounds."[4] "Everyone's a monster here,"[5] sighs Marielle, watching the passers-by from the Flore terrace… The *folles* of yesteryear, insufferable and delicious, have indeed disappeared. And with them, all of the "adventures of [Copi's] youth."[6] The show is over. All that remains is to kiss Marielle goodbye, grab a suitcase, and get off the stage in order to avoid crying, as we await the next episode in the fabulous and terrifying history of homosexuality.

THIBAUD CROISY

1. *Ibid.*, 155.
2. *Ibid.*, 153.
3. *Ibid.*, 156.
4. *Ibid.*, 149.
5. *Ibid.*, 9.
6. *Ibid.*, 148.

Index of Places

A chronicle of its time, *The Queens' Ball* invites the reader to stroll the streets of Paris and discover its most emblematic venues. These cafés, bars, restaurants, cabarets, clubs, and discotheques trace a map of Parisian desire and nightlife. Though most have disappeared and their names may mean little to today's reader, they are nonetheless significant to the narrative's economy. In fact, the narrator's itinerary shows him being torn between neighborhoods reflecting two different homosexual traditions: on the one hand, the "village" of Saint-Germain-des-Prés (6th arrondissement), where postwar homosexuals congregated and which Copi frequented in the early 1960s; on the other hand, Rue Sainte-Anne (1st and 2nd arrondissements), gay life's new epicenter, whose trendy clubs foreshadow the nightclubs of the 1980s. And this is precisely where Copi's journey ends, on a dance floor where he too feels "old"... Here is an overview of these fine addresses, whose shimmering colors shape the kaleidoscopic ball.

Café de Flore, 172 Boulevard Saint-Germain (6th). A world-renowned emblem of Parisian intellectual life. Huysmans, Apollinaire, André Breton, Georges Bataille, Robert Desnos and Pablo Picasso all went there. Jean-Paul Sartre,

Simone de Beauvoir and the existentialists made it their HQ. In the 1950s, Le Flore was also a meeting place for homosexuals. *Folles* flaunted themselves on the terrace and occupied the entire second floor. On his arrival to Paris, Copi smoked fine hash cigarettes there with Argentine painter Antonio Seguí (1934-2022). The café still exists today.

Chez Lipp, 151 Boulevard Saint-Germain (6th). An emblematic brasserie of Saint-Germain-des-Prés, inaugurated in 1880. Ceramics, paintings, maroon moleskin banquettes. A clientele of writers, poets, and politicians. The Prix Cazes, awarded to a writer who has previously not won a prize, is awarded there each year. The restaurant still exists today.

Le Fiacre, 4 Rue du Cherche-Midi (6th). Homosexual bar-restaurant with an international reputation. A must in the 1950s. It was run by Louis Baruc, a moustachioed, effeminate homosexual nicknamed "Loulou" or "Louise." On the first floor, Le Fiacre is frequented almost exclusively by young men. Upstairs, the restaurant is more mixed.

La Pergola, 1 Rue du Four (6th). A brasserie in Saint-Germain-des-Prés with an upper floor overlooking the neighborhood. As night falls, the clientele gives way to the night owls and gigolos who meet there before going to the Fiacre, Régine, or Castel.

Chez Régine, 1 Rue du Four (6th). Beneath the Pergola. A legendary club created in 1956, whose guests have included Françoise Sagan, Brigitte Bardot, and Rudolf Nureyev. It was run by Régine (1929-2022), a legendary nightclub owner who opened some twenty discotheques around the world. A singer—Serge Gainsbourg wrote lyrics for her, including the

legendary "Les femmes, ça fait pédé" (Women look like fags)—
she went on to become a gay icon. After Rue du Four, she
moved to Montparnasse (14th), where she opened New Jimmy's.

Chez Castel, 15 Rue Princesse (6th). Club-discotheque
founded in 1962 by Jean Castel, Régine's great rival. An
extremely chic gourmet restaurant housed in a hôtel partic-
ulier. A beacon of Parisian nightlife, Castel attracted the
likes of Sacha Distel, Jacques Dutronc, Françoise Hardy,
the singer Antoine, and Jacques Chazot... There, discreet
homosexuals mingled with a predominantly heterosexual
clientele. The club still exists today.

L'Alcazar, 62 Rue Mazarine (6th). Cabaret by Jean-Marie
Rivière and Marc Doelnitz. People came here to see trans-
formist numbers, enchanting revues, and feathered spectacles. As a Marilyn Monroe look-alike, Marie France was
the star of the show.

La Coupole, 102 Boulevard du Montparnasse (14th). A cele-
brated Art Deco brasserie inaugurated in 1927 and one of
Montparnasse's great landmarks. Regulars have included
Alberto Giacometti, Man Ray, Pablo Picasso, Yves Klein,
and Ernest Hemingway. In the 1970s, the "Coupole gang"
(Bulle Ogier, Pierre Clémenti, Jean-Pierre Kalfon) were also
to be seen there, along with Marie France, Alain Pacadis,
and Yves Adrien. Copi ordered platters of oysters and paid
the bill for everyone. The restaurant still exists today.

La Mendigotte, 80 Quai de l'Hôtel-de-Ville (4th). Restaurant, bar-club and discotheque. Young, gay clientele
surrounded by "fag hags."

Le Pimm's, 3 Rue Sainte-Anne (1st), et Le Club Sept, 7 Rue Sainte-Anne (1st). Establishments run by Fabrice Emaer, a legendary nightclub owner who enjoyed huge success when he opened Le Palace in 1978, just under a year after the publication of *The Queens' Ball*. Le Pimm's was a modern bar frequented by a gay clientele. Next door, Le Sept was the largest gay club in the neighborhood. On the first floor: a chic restaurant for the jet-set and intelligentsia (Andy Warhol, Roland Barthes, Yves Saint Laurent, and Grace Jones...), where a few gigolos in search of a Pygmalion also hung about. In the basement: a vaulted cellar with multicolored neon lights and mirror-covered walls. Despite the high prices, the owner, "Fabrice," was determined to make Le Sept a warm and open place, capable of competing with Régine and Castel, which were much more selective at the entrance. He experimented with mixing registers, which was to become the great Palace formula.

Le César, 4 Rue Chabanais (2nd). Bar-discotheque in the Sainte-Anne district run by a lesbian couple. Reserved for homosexuals of both sexes. The story of the valet dancing the paso doble was an inside joke Copi wrote for the bar's regulars. Spanish servants used to dance there and the customers would make fun of them. The establishment still exists today.

Continental-Opéra, 32 Rue Louis Legrand (2nd). One of the largest 1970s saunas, open day and night. The facilities included bars, pools, tanning and weight rooms. An innovation of the time with an avant-garde 1980s touch.

T. C.

Notes

[page 1]
…I always write with a Bic* pen…

Bic: In French, the Bic ballpoint pen is a masculine noun. Copi, on the other hand, makes it feminine, which brings "Bic" closer to the feminine noun "*bite*," the French word for "dick." In this light, Copi is punning on the possibility of "*writing with one's dick*." [An overwrought translation possibility would be: "the Dic pen."—Ed.]

…staged by Lavelli*…

Jorge Lavelli (1931-2023): an Argentine director born in Buenos Aires, who arrived in Paris in 1960. He made his name with the production of Witold Gombrowicz's *The Marriage*. When *The Queens' Ball* appeared, he had already directed three plays by Copi: *La Journée d'une rêveuse* (A dreamer's day) (1968), *L'Homosexuel ou la difficulté de s'exprimer* (1971), and *Les Quatre Jumelles* (The four twins) (1973). He was a member of the nebulous group of "Argentines in Paris" who delighted French audiences from the 1970s to the 1990s. He went on to become the director of the Théâtre national de la Colline in Paris (1987-1996), the small auditorium of which was inaugurated with Copi's last play: *Une Visite inopportune* (An inopportune visit).

[p. 6]
...I had to make a stop in Milan to see my dear friends the Gandinis...*

Giovanni Gandini (1929-2006): Milanese publisher. Founder of the Milano Libri publishing house (1962) and of the comics magazine *Linus*, where Copi's illustrations were featured. **Annamaria Gandini** was his wife. Gandini published one of Copi's finest collection of drawings, *Un livre blanc* (A white book) (1970), which he dedicated to both of them.

[p. 7]
And then it was off to the Tuileries, to make my first pickups who still stunk of aftershave.*

Jardin des Tuileries: the largest formal French-style garden in Paris, located between the Louvre and Place de la Concorde. To this day, the garden is a renowned cruising spot for gay men. Encounters take place in the bosquets on either side of the Arc de Triomphe du Carrousel.

[p. 8]
Marielle de Lesseps is sitting outside the Café de Flore.*

Marielle de Lesseps (1942-2001): great-granddaughter of Ferdinand de Lesseps (diplomat and entrepreneur who helped to develop the Suez Canal), cultural journalist for *Le Nouvel Adam*, *Le Nouvel Observateur*, *Le Matin de Paris*, and the radio program *Le Masque et la plume*. Intrepid and seductive, Marielle became friends with Copi in the 1960s. Appreciated in artistic and "trendy" circles, she preferred to hang about Saint-Germain-des-Prés and the terrace of Le Flore while her sister, Emmanuelle de Lesseps, was protesting in the ranks of the MLF (Women's Liberation Movement). Certainly one of the most beautiful characters found in Copi's novels.

[p. 9]
Staying with Julie Ann and Julian Cairol*,
whom she knows.

Julian Cairol (1930-2015): Copi's friend in early adulthood, born in Córdoba (Argentina). He lived in Boston with his wife, **Julie**. Copi's play *Eva Perón* was dedicated to him.

Wolinski and Sempé* are eating at the next table over.

Georges Wolinski (1934-2015), known as Wolinski, and **Jean-Jacques Sempé** (1932-2022), known as Sempé: French press cartoonists. The former is known for his subversive drawings in *Charlie Mensuel, Hara-Kiri* (where Copi was also a contributor), and *Charlie Hebdo*. The latter is a world-renowned cartoonist whose drawings combine humor, poetry, and gentle irony.

[p. 11]
I [...] go to a hotel on Boulevard Magenta*.

In the 10th arrondissement, far from the gay districts, **Boulevard de Magenta** links Place de la République to Boulevard

Barbès. By moving there, the narrator leaves the center of Paris and "provincializes" himself. For Copi, writing was often synonymous with travel. By writing, the author (re)becomes a foreigner, even if he remains in his own country.

[p. 29]
...I fix myself up a cup of Viandox* in what's left of my kitchen...

Viandox: a brand of savory sauce brand made from beef extracts, diluted in a bowl of hot water to make a broth. In the 1960s, it was often ordered in Parisian brasseries.

[p. 33]
Suddenly, I sit bolt upright in the taxi, cracking her whole scheme just as we pull up to Orly*.

Orly: The international airport that is closest to Paris.

[p. 44]
She is not bad, she is only interested on your shoe, Marilyn-Garbo says in English with an accent like Maurice Chevalier.*

Maurice Chevalier (1888-1972): one of the most famous French music-hall singers. With his boater hat, bow tie, and deliberately heavy Parisian accent, he was the epitome of passé French culture. To imagine "Marilyn-Garbo" speaking English with a Maurice Chevalier accent suggests she is unable to conceal her French origins. A charming massacre.

[p. 69]
...I see the whole old guard of Le Carrousel, Leslie's,
and Madame Arthur* walk the aisle in my house...

Transvestite cabarets which were inaugurated in the post-war years: in 1946 for **Madame Arthur**, which was founded by Marcel Wutsman (known as Monsieur Marcel) at 75 bis Rue des Martyrs, Pigalle; in 1947 for **Le Carrousel de Paris**, which was opened by Giuseppe Abatino and Joséphine Baker at 6 Rue Vavin. Madame Arthur still exists today, but as a tourist version that is quite far from the original cabaret.

[p. 73]
Marielle has access to all the telex* info.

Telex: Telegraph service. At the time, news agencies sent continuous information to newspaper editorial offices via telexes, which were printed on paper.

[p. 78]
Mme Audieu's favorite is Martine Carol*...

Marie-Louise Mourer, alias **Martine Carol** (1920-1967): the most popular French actress of the 1950s, eclipsed by Brigitte Bardot and now forgotten. Copi often quoted her. A platinum blonde and sort of proto-Marilyn Monroe, she played fallen courtesans or gentle fisherwomen in films with a tinge of eroticism. Max Ophüls offered her the lead role in *Lola Montès* (1955).

...a very fine actress who has since passed,
Tania Balachova...*

Tania Balachova (1902-1973): Russian-born French actress who performed for Antonin Artaud, Charles Dullin, Louis Jouvet, and Claude Régy, among others... She debuted the role of Inès in Jean-Paul Sartre's *No Exit* and played Solange in Genet's *The Maids*. A renowned teacher, she trained generations of artists and inspired Lee Strasberg, who founded the Actors Studio.

I walk down Strasbourg and Sébastopol*...*

Abbreviations for **Boulevard de Strasbourg** and **Boulevard de Sébastopol**. These two thoroughfares, which are in continuation with one another, link the center of Paris to the northern districts in a straight line.

Where'd Michou go, and La Grande Eugène*?*

Michel Catty, alias **Michou** (1931-2020): manager of the Cabaret Michou, located at 80 Rue des Martyrs in Pigalle, just opposite Madame Arthur. There, transvestites performed classic French songs (by Dalida, Édith Piaf, Sylvie Vartan). In the 1970s, with his kitsch style and bleached hair, Michou rose to stardom. He was a regular guest on both television and radio programs, where he embodied the worldly Montmartre gay man that all grandmothers adored. His cabaret still exists today.

La Grande Eugène, whose real name was Eugène Couvri (1941-1975), was a transvestite who performed at the eponymous cabaret. In his white feathered dress and wearing false teeth, he performed an unforgettable imitation of Mistinguett, the music-hall queen of the Roaring Twenties. He died at the age of thirty-three, just before the publication of *The Queens' Ball*. He had been offered the title role of Eva Perón in Copi's play, which was eventually played by Facundo Bo.

[p. 152, 153]

...they're thinking of marrying an old gay couple from the Arcadie* group that's been courting them for a while now, they'll pool their four pensions and spend their days raising pheasants to hunt in the Gâtinais*...

Association Arcadie: In reference to the Greek *Arkadía*, this was the name of a militant group founded in 1954 by André Baudry. It sought to promote respectable homosexuality through a reserved and discreet attitude. It used the word "homophile" instead of "homosexual" to emphasize the love, rather than sexual relations, between men. In the 1970s, Arcadie was marginalized by the more offensive and carnivalesque Front homosexuel d'action révolutionnaire (FHAR). By imagining Arcadie members in the **Gâtinais** countryside south of Paris, Copi mocked the older has-been homosexuals.

[p. 153]

...he's [...] waiting for the first Sunday morning metro to go back to the staff house where he lives in Neuilly*...

195

Neuilly: A residential community to the east of Paris. The epitome of a chic, conservative suburb.

[p. 155]
...I'm not particularly interested in going to Hôtel-Dieu*
at 5 a.m. to get stitches on my anus.

Hôtel-Dieu: Paris's oldest hospital, located on the Île de la Cité next to Notre-Dame Cathedral.

[p. 157]
...I head off toward my editor's on Rue Garancière*

Rue Garancière: a street in the 6th arrondissement near the Église Saint-Sulpice, where the offices of Christian Bourgois were located. The exact address (8 Rue Garancière) appeared on the title page of the original edition of *The Queens' Ball*. With his white hair and spectacles, the publisher's character was an explicit reference to Christian Bourgois (1933-2007), Copi's editor with whom he had a passionate and vaudevillian relationship. Most notably, Copi criticized Bourgois for not selling enough of his books, which is no doubt why he thought of killing him off in the sauna at Opéra and suggested that a *folle* come and "shit on his face"... before resurrecting him. For more on Copi and Christian Bourgois, see: Thibaud Croisy, "Copi ou la difficulté de l'éditer" (Copi, or the Difficulty of Editing Him), *Trou noir*, April 28, 2022, *https://www.trounoir.org/?Copi-ou-la-difficulte-de-l-editer-par-Thibaud-Croisy.*

I drop by the pissoir* at Place Saint-Sulpice,
someone's inside, I wait for him to finish, dump
Pierina in the urinal, and go on my way.

Pissoir, or *pissotière*: free male public outdoor bathrooms with teapot-shaped urinals. Installed in Paris as early as 1834, they were meeting spots for both homosexuals and prostitutes. Paris was long known for its countless public bathrooms until they were destroyed in 1980 and replaced with paying toilets. Today, only one remains on Boulevard Arago, near the Santé Prison (14th arrondissement). It pays unintentional tribute to the title of the final chapter of Copi's novel.

T. C.

—

COPI, whose given name was Raúl Damonte, was born in Buenos Aires, Argentina in 1939 and emigrated to Paris, France in 1962, where he died in 1987. He was a prolific playwright, novelist, and cartoonist whose provocative output thumbs its nose at modesty and melancholy. A canonical figure of 1970s Parisian bohemia and counterculture, he produced a prolific body of work that was hybrid and overflowing, ferocious and tender, baroque and distinct from the literary scene of his time. Among his most famous works are *The Queens' Ball*, *The Homosexual or the Difficulty of Sexpressing Oneself*, *Loretta Strong*, and *An Inopportune Visit*, known as the first play written in the French language to deal with the AIDS crisis. The unforgettable comics he published in major French outlets such as *Le Nouvel Observateur*, *Libération*, and *Hara-Kiri* are still widely circulated today.

KIT SCHLUTER was born in Boston in 1989. He has translated numerous books from the Spanish and French, including Marcel Schwob's *Book of Monelle* and Rafael Bernal's *His Name Was Death*, and is author of *Cartoons*, a collection of absurdist short stories and drawings, and *Pierrot's Fingernails*, a book of poems. He lives in Mexico City.

THIBAUD CROISY is an author and theater director. In recent years, he has staged several original plays, including *Témoignage d'un homme qui n'avait pas envie d'en castrer un autre* (Testimony of one man who didn't feel like castrating another man), *La Prophétie des Lilas* (The lilac prophecy), and *D'où vient ce désir, partagé par tant d'hommes, qui les pousse à aller voir ce qu'il y a au fond d'un trou?* (Wherefrom this desire, shared by so many men, to go see what's at the bottom of a hole?). In 2022, he directed Copi's *The Homosexual or the Difficulty of Sexpressing Oneself*, which was staged in Paris, Marseille, Nantes, Geneva, and elsewhere. He has written numerous texts on Copi, as well as afterwords to several recent editions of his works, and is currently preparing a Copi biography, forthcoming from Christian Bourgois éditeur.

OLIVIA BAES is a French-American multidisciplinary artist based in Catalonia. Her translations include Marguerite Duras' *The Easy Life* and *Me & Other Writing*, co-translated with Emma Ramadan. She is developing her first feature film, *Sirena*, with 15L Films, and is curator of the James Baes Foundation.

COPI DRESSED AS "L." FROM HIS PLAY,
LE FRIGO [THE FRIDGE].

PHOTOGRAPH BY JORGE DAMONTE (1983).